When the Boys Ran the House

OTHER YEARLING BOOKS YOU WILL ENJOY:

When the Boys Ran the House

by Joan Carris

illustrations by Carol Newsom

A YEARLING BOOK

Published by
Dell Publishing
a division of
The Bantam Doubleday Dell Publishing Group, Inc.
666 Fifth Avenue
New York, New York 10103

ISBN: 0-440-49450-8

Reprinted by arrangement with J. B. Lippincott Junior Books,
a division of Harper & Row, Publishers, Inc.

Printed in the United States of America

December 1983

10 9 8 7 6

CW

For my boys,
Tup and Tom and Tim,
Brad, Matt, Mark, Todd, and Drew

Contents

1   A Crazy Idea   *1*

2   Amazon Brown   *8*

3   Trouble   *19*

4   And More Trouble   *26*

5   Colorful Eleanore   *34*

6   Mister Justin Howard   *41*

7   Twinkies, Ring Dings, and
    Root Beer   *50*

8   Gus's Fissy   *63*

9   Time Out   *72*

10   Man the Mops   *85*

11   Marty the Hunter   *95*

12   Birds and Vegetables   *106*

13   The Awful Smell   *123*

14   Jut Tries Out   *136*

15   Jut Retires   *143*

1

A Crazy Idea

"Well, everybody's gone," Jut announced as he joined his three younger brothers at the kitchen table. They were having an after-dinner snack.

"Yay! They're gone!" cheered Nick, who was seven. He reached across Jut to Gus's highchair. "Gimme another cracker, Gus."

"No, no!" scolded Gus. At two, Gus told everyone no, no. He clutched all of his crackers to his chest.

"Quiet down," Jut warned in a worried tone. "You'll wake Mom. Her room's right above this one, remember? Dr. Collins said she needs plenty of sleep to get better."

"How long is she going to be sick, Jut?" Marty wrinkled his nose to adjust his glasses. "How long do we have to run the house?"

"I don't know. Before she left, Aunt Martha said Mom might have to stay in bed four or five weeks."

"Aunt Martha's stinky," Nick inserted. "I'm glad she's gone. We can have more fun alone." Nick grabbed one of the crackers Gus had put back down on his tray.

"NO, NO!" Gus shouted. "Bad baby!" He frowned at Nick and bent over the crackers on his highchair tray.

"Get your own crackers, Nick." Jut leaned back, balancing his chair on two legs. "Well, what do we want to do?"

"How about fishing?" suggested Nick.

"Nah," vetoed Marty. "All we'll get now is crawdads. Always by the time school starts the fish have left our creek and gone into the river."

"Monopoly?" Nick asked hopefully.

"Do not pass GO. Do not collect two hundred dollars," Marty intoned.

2

"Did you know," Jut interrupted, "that all those places on the Monopoly board are real streets in Atlantic City, New Jersey?" Jut collected odd facts.

"Oh, yeah?" Marty turned from Jut to Nick. "No Monopoly, Nick. I only like Monopoly with kids my age." He ran a hand through his brown, curly hair. "What are we going to do, anyway? This is boring, Jut."

Jut cleared his throat, but he couldn't think of a good answer. He looked from Marty, who was ten, and two and a half years younger than he, to Nick, who was making a face at Marty, and then to Gus, who was stuffing crackers in his mouth. Marty was right. Sitting at the kitchen table was boring. But was it up to *him* to think of something? Just because he was the oldest?

"I'm gonna go see Mom," Nick said.

"No you don't!" Jut countered quickly. He reached out and grabbed the back of Nick's shirt. "We have to stay away so she can sleep. Dr. Collins said so."

"I wanta see Mom!" Nick insisted, his voice tearful and angry at the same time.

"We aren't supposed to BOTHER MOM!" Marty hollered at Nick.

Jut winced. He let go of Nick's shirt and waved his hands in the air like their dad did when he wanted silence. "*Quiet*, you guys! Mom's sleeping, remember? Let's just go for a bike ride, okay?" Jut slid Gus's highchair tray forward so that he could lift Gus free of the chair.

"I haffa peepee," Gus said when he was standing up.

"I'll take him, Jut," Marty volunteered. "You want me to ride Mom's bike when we go so Gus can have his special seat?"

Jut knew how much Marty hated riding a girl's bike. "Thanks, but that's a big bike. I'll do it."

"I haffa peepee," Gus said again as a puddle grew between his sneakered feet.

"Aw, *rats*!" Marty made a face as he looked down at Gus.

"Hee, heee, heee," giggled Nick, pointing to Gus's embarrassment on the kitchen floor.

Gus frowned at Nick. Then he looked up at Jut. "Bad baby?" he asked softly.

"Right!" Jut groaned. "Geez, Gus, now somebody's got to wipe it up. Yech!" Jut had changed many diapers, but he had never learned to like it. A puddle of the stuff was even worse. He wished Gus were not being trained to a toilet—at least not now.

"How about if we draw straws?" Jut suggested.

"Forget it!" Marty said as he backed away from the puddle.

Nick was holding his nose. He made loud, gagging sounds as he retreated toward the front hall.

"Marty!" Jut's voice had authority. "You take him upstairs and change his pants. *I'll* wipe it up . . . *this time.*" Jut glared at Nick. "And can the noise!"

Being outside in the clear October air and riding a bike felt great. Jut breathed in the welcome coolness that had finally come to southern Ohio.

He checked behind him to make sure that Gus was safe in his seat above the rear fender. Ahead of him, Marty led the way down Center

Street toward the edge of town where they could ride around the park until dusk. Nick pedaled right behind Marty, arguing that he, Nick, ought to be in the lead.

"Boy, I don't know," Jut said out loud. "Dr. Collins said it was crazy to think we could manage things for several weeks. I just don't know."

2

Amazon Brown

"Well, Jut, you've survived a night and a morning. What do you think? Can we make it alone?" Mrs. Howard's voice was weak. She looked exhausted as she lay back against her pillows.

"Sure," Jut said, fast, before he let himself think. "No sweat." He knew his voice lacked enthusiasm, but he couldn't help it. He was too worried about his mother to feel enthusiastic. He wasn't sure Dr. Collins knew what he was doing. And he wasn't sure he wanted to be in charge for so many weeks.

"What's bothering you, Justin? I'm weak,

but not stupid. Don't you think we can do it?" Her voice sounded stronger. Her dark eyes were just as keen as ever.

"Uh, yeah . . . we can do it," Jut began, then stopped. "But what about you? When're you going to be able to get up? What is this sickness anyhow?"

"It's a type of encephalitis, Jut, an inflammation in my head—around the brain. That's why my head hurts all the time and why I had that fever for so long. But I'm getting better, especially now that I'm home from the hospital. I only wish Martha could have stayed longer, but she has to take care of her own family."

"Aunt Martha didn't want to stay any longer. Nick made her mad saying *ain't* all the time and singing those songs. You know how he does to get grownups mad?"

"Mmhmm, I sure do," Jut's mother nodded, smiling. "I suppose he *treated* her to some of his new swear words, too." Her smile faded.

"He sure did. And Marty's bugs got out, so one morning she woke up with his new yellow spider on her arm. *Killed* it, too. Marty told her she was mean to murder his newest spider."

"Mmhmm," Mrs. Howard said again.

"It's better for her to go back to Indianapolis," Jut summed up. "We were a pain for Aunt Martha."

Mrs. Howard bristled. "Sometimes, *Aunt Martha* is a pain. I love her, but it's a good thing *her* children happen to be two girls who like wearing clean clothes. You guys are *lots* more fun!"

"Thanks," he said. As long as his mom could think like that, she was really all right. Dr. Collins wasn't a dodo, and before long she'd be in charge again, just like always.

"Now, business. We have this morning to sort things out. Did Mrs. Thomas come for Gus right after breakfast?"

"She got him before breakfast. She said it was too hard for us to get ready for school and feed Gus too. She's coming every day at seven, she said."

"Bless her," said Jut's mother. "We couldn't do this without her. And she's bringing him home around four or five?"

Jut nodded. "She's bringing your lunch all week until you're up more, too."

"She's *wonderful*. Now, how about the boys? Did they get off for school okay?"

"Sorta. Marty keeps bossing Nick around—being the big cheese. Nick's getting worse and worse. Said he wouldn't feed Eleanore. Isn't that dumb?"

Mrs. Howard smiled. "No. Nick knows that whoever takes care of that cat has to clean her kitty litter. I'll ask Marty to look after Eleanore. She's always liked him. But whoever's been feeding her lately has given her too much food. She's looking rather chubby."

"Oh, she's okay," Jut said. He whipped out his favorite book from his back pocket. "*Guinness* says the fattest house cat weighed forty-two pounds." He grinned at his mother. "Eleanore's a midget compared to that!"

"I don't care what your book says. Eleanore's been making a pig of herself. You guys should cut back on her food." She yawned and stretched against her pillows. "Let's finish so you can get off to school. I told your principal you'd be in by ten o'clock. How about Pierpont? Are you watching him?"

Jut laughed at the idea. Pierpont was the Howards' old basset hound. He moved as slowly as he could. It took him five minutes to decide that, yes, the door to the backyard was open, and yes, maybe he would go over to the door . . . then amble through it . . . and then sit down on the top step to look over the yard.

"Anybody who 'watches' Pierpont would go to sleep," Jut said. "Don't worry about this kind of stuff, Mom. I can handle it." Now that he wasn't afraid of his mother's sickness, Jut felt he could do anything . . . well, *almost* anything.

"Just see me if there're problems. The visiting nurse comes today, and Wednesdays, and Fridays. Dr. Collins said he'd stop in every other day on his way home. And I've got Gramma Howard's bell so I can call you all home any time I need to." She motioned to the heavy rope that ran from her bedpost across the room and out the window. The rope continued on till it reached Gramma Howard's antique bell that stood on a post beside the front porch.

"That bell rope was a great idea. Uncle Jut said yesterday that he had to do something since he couldn't stay and take care of us."

"He's my favorite brother-in-law," said Mrs. Howard. "But we don't need someone here now, Jut. We'll be fine. Who cares if meals are a little odd for a few weeks or if dust collects on tables?"

"Right! And nobody's going to write Dad? It's still a secret?"

"You bet it is! He'd come charging home if he knew I was sick, and lose his chance to make all those sales. Nope; *nobody's* going to mess up all those years of his work and planning."

Jut understood. Mr. Howard had left a large computer company and gone into business for himself several years ago. And now he'd been asked to demonstrate his own computers and their programs at several businesses in Europe. He had planned carefully to include all of those businesses in one trip. He'd be gone for several more weeks.

"We can do it," Jut said, his mood light. "It'll be kind of fun to fix meals and pick out groceries and stuff. And Marty wants to help.

He really does." Jut remembered Marty's offer to pedal the girl's bike that had Gus's seat attached. He'd been surprised by Marty's helpfulness, in fact. *But I always think of Marty arguing with Nick,* Jut told himself. *Or running around with a bug jar. Or reading.* Jut realized that maybe he didn't *know* Marty—not really.

"I'm sure Martin will be helpful," Mrs. Howard said. "Why don't I suggest that he be half the cheese? You run some things and let him manage others? Then nobody works all the time."

"*Marty* run things?" Jut thought about the idea. "Yeah, sure. He'd like that, and I could keep Nick busy. That'd cut down some of the fights."

"Exactly. Well, we sound pretty organized. You'd better get on to school before it gets any later. I have to sleep another ten or twenty hours." She smiled and punched her pillow into position. "Keep an eye out for Miss Brown, the visiting nurse. She's due here between three and four o'clock."

Jut put Pierpont and Eleanore in the backyard before he left for school. The dog and cat would stay outdoors, he knew, for most of the morning. Then they'd come inside by way of their pet door for an afternoon nap. "Mom's right," he said to Eleanore as she jounced past him and the doddering Pierpont. "You are getting fat."

Jut jogged down the street to Hampshire Junior High. Eighth grade wasn't bad, he had decided. They had a good basketball team in his school and a great track team. He knew he wasn't fast enough for track, but he hoped to make the basketball team. Tryouts were in November, and Jut had spent many summer hours in practice for those tryouts. But he was short for basketball. Some tall creep would probably edge him out and then he wouldn't be part of any team at all.

The day in school went fast. It'd be nice, he thought, if every school day could begin at ten o'clock. That way, he missed Ohio history and English. Miss Twilley, who taught English, was Jut's least favorite teacher of all time. She never seemed to notice when the girls were talking, but just let a boy lean across the aisle to whisper to another boy, and

15

whammo! She had made him stay after school for talking twice already and it was only the beginning of October.

Jut dashed out of school the second the bell rang so that he'd be home first. He had barely gotten inside the house when the front doorbell rang. The ring was followed by brisk knocking.

Jut opened the front door and started looking up. Immaculate white met his eyes; next a gold medical pin; then a young, tanned face. A peaked, rigidly starched cap rode atop reddish curls. The cap was slightly crooked, as though it had trouble staying in place.

"Uh, how do you do." Jut swallowed. He dropped his eyes to his sneakers while he tried to guess how tall the nurse was. This had to be Nurse Brown, but who'd have guessed there'd be so much of her? She was six feet two, maybe, or three? She was an Amazon! When he looked up, she was looking down at him.

"I'm six feet, *four* inches tall. Don't mess with me, kid. I used to play basketball in college and I'm *mean!*" She tried not to grin, but couldn't help herself.

16

"G-great!" Jut stammered. *Basketball*. "Do you think you could, uh . . . give me a few pointers? I want to make the team in November, but I'm short so I have to be good. I mean, *really good*."

"I saw that hoop over your garage doors. I'd be glad to help, but first lead me to your mom. She's famous. Haven't had a good case of encephalitis here in years. I'll see you in about forty-five minutes." She grinned again

17

and poked him in the chest on her way toward the steps upstairs.

While he waited for the nurse, Jut checked his record book. One woman on record was seven feet, five inches tall, a whole thirteen inches taller than Nurse Brown. He wondered if the nurse would like to know that. He began practicing baskets while he waited. Maybe he should get to know her better before he told her she was a shrimp.

A basketball-playing nurse sure was lucky. He could hardly wait to tell Marty. Maybe Marty would like to fix dinner, Jut thought as he caught the ball after a perfect lay-up. Somebody who was half the cheese would want to help cook—it was only logical.

3

Trouble

"Wait'll you see her, Marty." Jut was filling Marty and Nick in on the day's news, especially Nurse Amazon Brown, who was upstairs with their mother.

"I'm gonna go look at her," Nick decided.

"Later," Jut said. "Right now, let's empty the dishwasher. If we all help, it'll go fast and we can go play ball." The neighboring dead-end circle, Holly Tree Court, was known for its ballgames that went on forever.

Arms loaded with plates from the dishwasher, Jut nosed open the cupboard door. His eyes fastened on the air vent in the wall above the cupboard. A large bee sailed out of the vent and coasted around the kitchen ceiling. Another bee followed. And another. Jut froze, plates and job forgotten.

How could bees get inside the air vent? While Jut watched, four more bees followed their leader into the Howards' kitchen. Seven bees. Seven bees in less than a minute. Now Jut could *hear* bees, not just see them.

"Uh, Marty," he began.

"Yeah, I just noticed." Marty put the last of the clean knives into the silverware drawer. "They look good, too. Healthy. Must've had a great year." He watched the bees circle the ceiling.

"Aw, come off it, Marty! Bees in the house don't look good! How'd they get in here?"

Marty shrugged his shoulders and went on admiring the bee parade.

"I'm gonna murdalize 'em," hissed Nick. He advanced from the broom-closet corner and waved the fly swatter back and forth in the air.

"Oh no you're not!" Instantly, Marty was in charge. "Don't make 'em mad. Right now

20

they're okay. Confused, maybe, but okay. Make 'em angry and we've had it."

Jut gulped. He had gone through life ignoring bees. Bees had responded by ignoring Jut, and that was just how Jut wanted it. "What do we do?" he asked Marty, whispering and hating his nervousness.

"Close off the kitchen," Marty answered briskly, "and go outside to find out how they're getting in. Come on, Nick, outside!" Marty shut the doors from the kitchen into the other rooms. He shooed both Nick and Jut ahead of him into the garage.

Looking over the weathered house shingles, they saw a hole under one kitchen window. "Must be here," Marty said professionally. "They're making the hole bigger, and I hear lots of bee noises in there." He leaned over and put his ear next to the bee hole.

Jut backed away from Marty's heroism. "Geez," he whistled under his breath. "Don't get so close!"

"And what have we here?" asked Miss Brown.

"Wow!" Nick said. "She *is* a big one!"

21

I'm going to kill that kid, Jut said to himself. He felt the red heat of embarrassment as he turned to face the nurse. "Gee, Miss Brown," Jut began miserably.

"Never mind," Miss Brown chuckled. "It's the truth. And it's one reason I was such a good basketball player." She put her hands on her hips and bent down to look Nick right in the face. "Want to learn how to play basketball?" she asked him.

"Honest?" Nick asked, unbelieving. *"Me?"*

"Now's a *good* time. Except, first, what about that bee hole?"

"That's what we want to know," Marty answered. "They've found the way into our kitchen through the air ducts."

The nurse shook her head. "Old houses often have trouble with bees. Tonight, when they're all in there, spray that hole with poison. Then plug it up. They can't get out, so they'll have to die."

Marty shook his head doubtfully. "Bees're pretty tough. If they don't die, then they'll keep on coming into the house, right?"

"Wrong. I think they'll all die. If a few do find their way into the house, just swat them.

They'll be awfully sick, so they won't be able to fight back."

"Good!" Jut enjoyed hearing how sick the bees would get.

"Can we play basketball now?" Nick asked. He had moved to stand next to the nurse.

"Let's go," she said. "I have to see another patient before the afternoon's gone."

Miss Brown hadn't been kidding about knowing basketball. Jut watched, open-mouthed, as she dribbled the ball and made shot after shot effortlessly. Her ball never even kissed the rim. It swooshed through the exact center of the hoop. He had never played on the same court with perfection before.

"This is great," she said after several minutes. "Big flat piece of cement, and your hoop's at the perfect height. Come on, let's practice some lay-ups. You, too, Nick." She tossed the ball to Nick first.

"Put your hands like this," she said. "How those hands fit on the ball means a lot." Nick loved the attention she gave him.

Several minutes passed. The foursome on the court had an audience of only two: Pierpont and Eleanore. When Nick got tired of trying to heave the ball up to the basket, he became part of the audience in the grass. But Jut and Marty never tired of trying to shoot and move like Amazon Brown.

"Got to go now, sorry. I'll have more time Wednesday afternoon." She smoothed her uniform skirt and picked up her cap from the top of a shrub. Everyone followed her to the car, even the animals.

"Bye, Howards," she said. She ruffled Nick's hair, petted Pierpont, and scratched behind Eleanore's ears. "Bye, flabby tabby," she added, running her hands down Eleanore's back.

Jut and Marty laughed. It would be super, Jut thought, to have Nurse Brown to look forward to three afternoons a week.

"We have to put Eleanore on a diet," Jut said. "See you Wednesday."

Miss Brown threw her medical bag in the car and got in after it. "No diet gets rid of pregnancy," she teased as she began backing out of the driveway.

"No, no," Jut called after her. He felt funny talking about pregnancy with a lady he hardly knew. "The person we got her from said she'd been spayed. No kittens."

"Oh, yeah? Well, don't forget about the bee hole. Plug it up tonight when all the bees are home and snoring. Bye!" Her hand waved a long time, until her car was out of sight around the corner.

"Would a nurse know about bees?" Marty asked as they walked toward the house.

"How should I know?" Jut's answer was curt. Bees in the house, for cripes sake. Right off the bat something had to go wrong.

4

And More Trouble

"Can you fry eggs?" Marty asked Jut.

Jut poured the third bowl of cereal and sat down at the breakfast table. "I suppose. Why?"

"I'm sick of cereal, that's why," Marty said. "And I'm sick of peanut butter and jelly, too. Can't we do better at fixing meals?"

Jut nodded happily at Marty. Great. He hadn't remembered to ask Marty if he'd do some cooking. Now Marty had thought about it and he thought it was all his idea. "Okay," he said. "You plan some good meals and then you can cook them."

26

"Eggs stink," Nick commented as he poured milk on his cereal.

Marty started to answer, but clamped his mouth shut while he watched something. He watched for several minutes, then cleared his throat loudly.

Jut looked up from the toast he was coating with peanut butter.

"Look at that!" Marty pointed a finger. "I knew it! All dead, huh?"

Jut followed Marty's finger to a point in midair where a lazy-looking bee floated. Again, Jut felt his unwelcome fear, and the anger because he was afraid of something so little. Something that didn't faze Marty. Something that told him he wasn't in charge of things like he was supposed to be. "What now?"

"Murdalize 'em!" Nick waved the fly swatter.

"*I'll* do that!" Marty snatched the swatter out of Nick's hand and killed the bee. "He was sick anyway. That poison we sprayed in their hole will make them all sick. Do you see any more?" Marty tapped the swatter on the knee of his jeans. "Probably be a few more come in here. *Just like I thought,*" he added knowingly.

For the rest of breakfast, everyone watched for bees. Two more drifted out of the air vents. Marty killed them swiftly. "I *knew* it," Marty said each time he finished off a bee.

"What about Mom?" Jut asked. "What if more come in and bother her while we're at school?"

"She sleeps all the time. She won't even see 'em . . . I hope. Maybe, after school, we can spray more poison in their hole." Marty piled books into his backpack. "We'll close off the kitchen, though, so any bees that come in will stay right here."

Within minutes they were ready to leave for school. No more bees came into the kitchen, much to Nick's disgust. He had said it was HIS turn to kill bees so many times that Jut had finally agreed. Only there weren't any more bees. All the way to school, Nick scowled at Marty and called him a hoggy know-it-all.

Jut raced home from school for the second day in a row. Somehow, he felt he ought to be there when Nick and Marty came home. He opened the back door leading into the kitchen and gasped in shock.

The kitchen was solid bees. They were on every surface. They filled the air.

Just looking at the bees in his kitchen made Jut sick—made him hate being the oldest. What if the bees were upstairs too? Nobody could sleep through that many bees. And what was he supposed to *do* about it?

"Well, go on in," Marty said, testily as he came up to the door. "I got a ton of home-work."

Jut let out the breath he hadn't known he was holding. "Geez, Marty, don't go in there! Place's stuffed with bees!"

Marty dropped his books with a loud thwack. "I knew it!" He wiggled his glasses into place and sat down on the steps next to Jut. "How do they look? Mad? Confused?"

Jut closed his eyes. "Who knows? I'm not the bugologist in this family! I hate bees, re-member?"

"I'll go in and check," Marty said reassur-ingly. "Just stay here and wait for Nick so he doesn't come in."

"You're crazy!"

"Maybe, but I want to fix something good for dinner so I need the kitchen. Those bees have gotta go."

Jut nodded numbly. But *how?* he asked himself. And now he wouldn't trade places with Marty for anything. In the past, Jut had sometimes wished he were Marty. That way he wouldn't be the oldest. And Marty was so sure about things. He had always known that someday he'd be a biologist or an entomologist. "Boy, not *me*," Jut said under his breath. Still, it would be nice to know what was coming next: what he would do with himself after high school.

"What's up?" Nick asked as he came into the garage.

"Marty's inside taking bees' pulses," Jut said gloomily. "Whole downstairs is full of bees." Jut hoped that would discourage Nick from going inside.

"Okay, then it's *my* turn to kill some. Like you promised this morning."

"No!" Jut snapped. "There're too many now. You'd get stung."

"I wanta kill bees," Nick insisted. He stuck out his jaw and glared at Jut.

"Forget it! You've been a brat since Mom got sick. Now shape up and shut up. We've got a problem!"

Nick was so surprised by Jut's outburst that he didn't say anything for a few seconds. Then he said, "You're gonna be sorry, Jut. I'm gonna *tell Mom*!" His chin was quivering.

Jut looked at Nick and for some reason he thought of their dad. Mr. Howard would not have lost his temper with Nick.

"Look, Nick. There's billions of bees in there. I don't want you to get hurt." Jut thought fast and reached for his pile of school books. "Here. Draw a picture about our bees. Mom'll like that. I'll let you use my new Magic Markers and paper from art class, okay?" Jut held out paper and Magic Markers.

Nick took the peace offering. "Maybe," he said. "Maybe I will and maybe I won't." He turned and left the garage.

"Geez!" Jut muttered as he watched Nick's stiff back march away.

Marty jumped out the back door and

slammed it shut behind him. "All set, Jut. Exterminator's coming today. Mom and I decided the bees were winning." Marty paused, then looked at Jut. "What's the matter? It's just a few bees . . . and they're not well bees . . . and they're not upstairs where Mom is." Marty shook his head. "You're taking all this too serious, Jut. Those bees are okay. Our poison made 'em all groggy, not mean."

"Groggy, huh? Well, when they're asleep *for good,* then I won't be so *serious!*"

Around five o'clock, the exterminator came in a bright yellow car. The car had black signs printed on it and looked like a bee on wheels.

Mrs. Thomas brought Gus home at the same time. Jut thanked her and took Gus to play in the sandbox until the house was empty of bees. While Jut and Gus buried ants in the sandbox, Pierpont dozed next to them in the grass. Neither Eleanore nor Nick was around.

Marty attached himself to the exterminator. "Can I ask you some questions, sir?" The exterminator nodded and let Marty carry the hoses for his bee poison.

After about an hour, the bee car pulled out

of the Howards' driveway. Marty came over to the sandbox where Jut and Gus were still holding ant funerals.

"Sure is a crime. Stuff costs forty dollars and it'll kill all the insects we've got for about three or four months!"

Jut could tell that Marty was disgusted with the extermination process. "I'll bet Mrs. Thomas'll let you collect bugs at her place, bet anything."

Marty gave Jut a relieved smile. "Sure, sure she would." He dusted his hands together briskly. "Well, gotta get to work on dinner. You can help, Jut, and Gus'll watch TV."

"TB! TB!" Gus rocked to his feet and began climbing out of the sandbox.

On the way to the house, Marty said, "Wait'll we tell that nurse how her idea *didn't work.*"

5

Colorful Eleanore

"What I meant about dinner," explained Marty, his head in the canned goods cupboard, "was a bunch of foods everybody liked. Like ravioli." He set out a can of ravioli. "And some black olives." He saw a bottle of pancake syrup and put it out too. "We could do some frozen waffles. Gus loves waffles."

Jut caught Marty's spirit. Now that the bees were gone, life looked good again. He decided to fix celery stuffed with peanut butter, his all-time favorite snack. Marty warmed several cans of food while Jut stuffed celery. Then, because stuffing was fun, Jut stuffed celery

34

with cheese spread. Like grouting between bathroom tiles, he thought, remembering one Saturday when he and his dad had repaired the upstairs bathroom floor.

Gus left the TV when news came on at six. He settled on the kitchen floor and began pulling pots and pans out of the cupboard. Marty fell over a skillet twice and then exploded. "Why does Mom let him *do* that?"

"Because he likes to play with real things, Mom said."

"Miaaaaow," begged Eleanore at the screen door. She had ignored her pet door and was asking to be let in.

Marty opened the door and Eleanore slunk in low, belly polishing the linoleum. Her ears lay flat against her head.

"Eleanore!" Marty let out a low whistle.

Jut turned to look and dropped the apple he was stuffing.

"Oh, *Eleanore.*" Marty sat down and coaxed the cat onto his lap. And then Marty read Eleanore.

On her tail she said SH——T in kelly green letters. Her right side said D——MN in vivid

35

purple, and her left side said H——L in fluo-rescent pink. Her head was blobbed with a black design that looked like a squashed spi-der.

"Magic Marker," breathed Marty.

"*Permanent* Magic Marker," Jut amended. "Nick must have done it, and *I* gave him the Magic Markers." Jut stared at his mother's cat.

"Funny how he *disguised* the words." Mar-ty's voice was heavy with sarcasm as he pointed to the missing vowel space on the cat's tail. Eleanore hunkered between Marty's legs and did not purr.

Jut looked at Marty then, and Marty re-turned the look. Both began to laugh. "A graf-fiti cat!" Jut roared.

"Yeah, an R-rated feline!"

Several minutes of hilarity went by. When Jut caught his breath, he said, "But what're we going to do with Nick?"

Marty's answer was prompt. "He has to be punished. I'm in charge of Mom's cat, and look what he did to her."

Jut felt like the oldest again. Somehow, he was sure that punishment wouldn't help anything. "If we sort of ignore it, it'd be better. He wants to get us mad. That's why he did it."

"How do you know that?"

"I *just do*. Look, Marty, I'll take the blame for it. Just stay out of it, okay? Nick's just waiting to fight with you, like always. So don't do it."

Marty shrugged. "Okay, but he's gettin' off easy, if you ask me."

"Go upstairs and tell Mom so she doesn't have a fit when she sees Eleanore. Maybe you ought to take her along—for show and tell." Jut grinned in spite of his worry over how to handle Nick.

But Eleanore wouldn't be taken anywhere. As Marty reached for her she slithered away and ran into the laundry room. They heard her pet door flap to and fro. She had gone outdoors.

"Cats *hate* to be laughed at," Marty said as he stood up. "I'll go tell Mom."

When Nick came home, no one said anything about Eleanore. Jut told Nick to get the Magic Markers and extra paper and put them where they belonged. That was all Jut said.

Dinner was a banquet. Marty had warmed spaghetti and meatballs as well as ravioli. There were black olives, which everyone liked, and no one said, "Stop eating all the olives."

Gus ate three toasted waffles with syrup. Jut ate all of the things stuffed with peanut butter. He had added apples to the celery. Nick and Marty said the cheese-stuffed celery was delicious.

For dessert they had banana splits because that was fruit as well as dessert, Jut said, and so it was healthy.

"Aaaarg, am I *full*," Marty groaned at the end of his banana split. "This was better, though, right? Better than peanut butter and jelly?"

"You're a *great cook*, Marty," Jut said, hoping that Marty would learn to love cooking. "Nick, take Gus outside and play with him while we clean up dinner."

Nick started to argue but Jut spoke quickly. "You *owe* us one, buddy. Now, *move*! And don't let him out of your sight. I'm going to watch from the window over the sink while I clean up."

Nick looked up at Jut respectfully. "Okay. Come on, Gus." Nick picked Gus up and lugged him over to the door. Nick was a thin boy and Gus a heavy toddler. Still, Nick always liked carrying Gus, even now when Gus could walk.

Jut and Marty started cleaning up the kitchen. "Peanut butter sandwiches are neater," Jut grumbled, scrubbing spaghetti off the pan bottom.

The creak of the Howards' twelve-year-old swing set came through the open window. Nick had put Gus on one side of the glider swing, and Nick was standing up, pumping the glider. This was how they played trolley car, Gus's favorite game.

"On top of the *schooooool*house," warbled Nick, "all covered with blood, I shot my poor *teeeeeee*chur, with a forty-foot slug.

"I shot her with *plehhhhh*zhure, I shot her with pride. I couldn't have *miiiiissed* her, she's forty feet wide."

Gus hummed along. He was Nick's biggest fan. Sometimes, he was Nick's only fan.

Inside, Marty scraped cat food from its can into Eleanore's bowl.

"Don't give her very much, Marty. She's eating like a pig lately."

6

Mister Justin Howard

"I promised I'd ask you to be his parent." Jut's mother looked as if she might go on begging him, but instead she said, "You know how he looks up to you, Jut. And he's having a rough time now, with Dad gone."

Jut sighed loudly. He knew he would do what his mother wanted, because she was counting on him. Absently, he petted Eleanore, who lay stretched out on Mrs. Howard's blanket.

"I guess," he said finally. "How long does Back-to-School Night last?"

"Just over an hour. And *thank you,* dear.

Nick will be *so* glad when you tell him."

Jut nodded and went on petting Eleanore. "She's thinner, don't you think. How'd you get her to come in? We haven't seen her around all week."

"Marty found her for me as a favor, but I still think you need to cut back on her food. She's not any thinner."

"Marty says she's hunting. He's seen her hunting."

A frown crossed Mrs. Howard's face. "Oh, boy, is that a sore subject."

"What subject?"

"Hunting. This is Marty's tenth fall, remember? Your father promised him he could go with you guys this year, and Marty hasn't forgotten."

Jut understood immediately. He remembered the fall he was ten and had gone hunting with his father for the first time. It was a special thing. Marty wouldn't forget.

"Squirrel season's opening soon. He could go with me. I'm a good hunter, just ask Dad."

"Dad and I will talk it over when he calls again so that I can give Marty an answer. I know you boys understand about gun safety, but *I* wasn't raised on an Iowa farm like your father, and hunting makes *me nervous!*"

Jut smiled reassuringly. "It'll work out, Mom, don't sweat it. Now tell me what I do for Back-to-School Night."

"My seat's in the front row," Nick called after Jut. "My name's on the desk. Look for the name tag I made for you, Jut."

"I know, I know! You've told me all this stuff, Nick. You mind Marty tonight, hear? That's our deal." He waved good-bye to Nick for the last time.

Jut hurried toward Nick's and Marty's school. As he jogged down the street he pushed and pulled at his clothes, hating the shirt collar and tie. "I don't know how Dad stands it," he said aloud. "Dumbest clothes ever invented."

Jut slowed down as he remembered that tonight he was taking the place of his dad. Thinking of fathers, he opened his records book. Lots about mothers, and a picture of the oldest mother and her kid. But no information about the youngest father on record. Not a peep. Not even a picture of the oldest father. Jut got sidetracked by the picture of the man with the longest fingernails. Somehow, whenever he opened the book he saw that picture. It made his stomach turn.

Jut entered the school just ahead of its principal, Mr. Rawson. He hoped to be ignored, but he wasn't.

"Good evening, Jut. Wish you'd tell your father for me, next time he calls, that we certainly miss him at the town council meetings. How's his trip going?"

"Fine, sir. He says it's a very lucrative trip." Jut was glad he'd remembered the exact word. Mr. Rawson was big on vocabulary.

Jut nodded good-bye to the principal as he stepped into Nick's classroom, where everything was as Nick had said. His name tag had been carefully, colorfully printed: MR. JUSTIN HOWARD. Each letter was a different color, like Eleanore, the graffiti cat. Jut grinned, remembering. The front-row desk, where he had to sit, was right under the teacher's eye.

Mrs. Connors, Nick's main teacher, stood up behind her desk, winked at Jut, and began explaining second grade to all of the parents. She introduced Nick's team of teachers. "In second grade," she said, "language arts are emphasized the most. For a change, we have a former pupil here who can tell us how *much* that helped him." She paused, then added, "I'm not going to consider the idea that he *wasn't* helped!" She smiled broadly around the room.

Then she looked at Jut. "Just take my place up here and tell us what you remember about second grade."

Appalled, Jut looked down at Nick's desk. He would *never, ever* have asked a kid to do that unless the kid had been told ahead of time.

Behind him, another voice spoke. It was Miss Feldstein, a golden memory from second grade. She was Nick's science teacher just as she had been Jut's. "Gut it out," she whispered sympathetically. "I know you can do it. A few sentences will be plenty."

Jut got to his feet inch by inch. He knew

that his book of world records made a bulge in his suit pants. And the pants were too short. He was wearing his go-to-church suit from seventh grade and it was too small.

It seemed hours later that he stood at Mrs. Connors' desk in front of everyone. All of the seats in the room were full. All of the people in the seats were looking right at him. He cleared his throat. "I, uh, I *do* remember second grade," he began.

Of course, much of what he remembered he couldn't tell. At least not to parents. You didn't tell parents that you waited for two o'clock every afternoon because that's when Janie Granger wet her chair. Jut sat next to her and knew when she'd used up her bathroom passes. That fact made her so nervous she wet her chair. It was always good for interrupting class.

Also, as the year went on, he and the other boys made bets with one another about whether she'd do it or not. One memorable day Jut had won four Oreos, a candy bar, and a fruit pie, betting on Janie Granger.

"Yes," Jut repeated, "I have many memories of second grade." He remembered when Tommy Newcombe had moved to Hampshire. The second-grade boys had given Tommy a special welcome that first day in the boys' bathroom. They'd taken all of his clothes, wadded them up in his T-shirt, and tossed the ball of clothing out the window. They had smiled at Tommy and said, "Hope you get to like it here in the john," and had run on back to class. That was long ago, and he and Tommy were good friends now.

It occurred to Jut that he was remembering only bathroom subjects. Was that how he thought of second grade?

"The, uh, the stories we read were good," Jut finally managed, tearing his thoughts away from the bathroom. He searched his memory. "I liked *Ramona*. And there was a super book about a boy who ate fifteen worms. Big ones. Big worms, I mean."

Mrs. Connors moaned.

"I," Jut coughed, "I probably read that one at home. But it was *great*. And we did a lot of spelling and writing." Jut took a deep breath. "I was awful at writing and I hated it. But that year I got better."

He decided he had said enough. "Thank you." He banged his leg on the corner of the desk as he hurried to sit down in Nick's seat.

The rest of the evening's talks went by in a blur. Jut hunkered in Nick's seat, eyes down, and thought of dozens of things he *could have* said. Good things, not bathroom stories or little, jerky sentences.

And then there were two strangers, one on each side of him. "Thank you," a woman said sincerely. "You told me exactly what I needed to know." She shook Jut's hand.

"Remember the title of that worm book?" A red-haired man grinned at Jut. "My boy would like that story."

"It's *How to Eat Fried Worms*. And it really *is* good." Jut sat up straighter.

"Thanks," said the man. "You coming to the gym for refreshments?"

Jut had planned to run home as soon as possible. Now he wasn't sure. "Gee, uh, what are the refreshments?"

"Cider and donuts." He motioned toward the door. "Almost makes it worth listening to the talks, see? Come on." He held out his hand. "Name's Greg Anders. I don't think we've met. My family's new in town."

"Pleased to meet you," Jut answered, shaking hands and giving his name. "We live in that real old house on Hillside, corner of Grove."

7

Twinkies, Ring Dings, and Root Beer

"How about a little game of HORSE?" Amazon Brown dribbled the ball lightly around Jut and Marty.

"Not me," panted Nick. "Me 'n' Pierpont'll watch." Nick flopped on the grass and pillowed his head on the sleeping hound.

Jut said, "Let me start. I'm going to pick all the hard shots on purpose, just so I have to practice them."

"Then I've had it," Marty said. "I'm not any good at basketball anyhow." His face was long.

"You're better than you were," Jut replied quickly. "Lots better. And it's nice to have somebody to practice with."

Marty brightened. "Okay, so I'll be a horse first—AGAIN!" He made a face at Jut and bounce-passed the ball to him fast.

Marty was right about losing. He missed shots that Jut and Amazon Brown made. First he was an H, then an O. Soon he was a whole HORSE. "That means *I* don't have to go to the grocery store," he said as he missed his last-chance shot.

"It *does*?" Jut tried a sweeping underhand shot and missed.

"Oh, ho! Getting sneaky, Mr. Howard." Amazon Brown's underhand soared upwards. It reached in an arc for the heavens, then came down through the center of the hoop.

"That's disgusting!" Jut said.

Miss Brown grinned. "Who's going to the store? Can I help?"

"No, thanks. We've made a list and we've got two bikes with big baskets. Mom and Dad often get the groceries on bikes because the store's close."

"And you *promised*!" threatened Nick from the sidelines. "You said I could help."

51

Jut said good-bye to any last hope of avoiding the grocery store. Marty and Nick fought too much to send them together. He would have to go. "Okay, Nick. As soon as I'm a horse."

"We can take care of that," Amazon Brown said, grinning at Marty and Nick.

Three minutes later, Jut was an official HORSE, and Amazon Brown was ready to leave. "Where's your fat cat? I haven't seen much of her lately."

Marty shot a worried glance at Jut. "We haven't either. That's weird, too, because she used to always stay with Mom. She's Mom's cat."

"Your mother is doing very well, by the way," Miss Brown said. "She'll be up for a little while each day now, but don't let her do anything. I'm sure her head still aches quite a bit, so just enjoy her company."

The nurse shut her car door and started the engine. "Oh, and something else." She paused. "I don't want to insult you, but there's a funny smell in your living room. I noticed it today when I came into the house."

"Funny smell?" Jut asked weakly. He hadn't thought about the possibility of funny smells. He had tried to think of everything. He had even done the laundry.

"Sort of . . . garbagy, if you know what I mean." She looked embarrassed. "Sorry," she added. "See you all on Friday."

Jut nodded and waved her out of the driveway. He closed his eyes and tried to imagine why there would be a smell in the living room.

"Bet it's my goldfish," Marty said suddenly. "I'll fix it, Jut. Let's get the grocery list, so you can do that. I'll take Gus when Mrs. Thomas brings him and clean my fishbowl."

Jut took his father's bike down from the hook where it hung in the garage. He wiped off some of the dust, then joined Nick, who was waiting with his bike in the driveway.

"Baskets are *baby*," Nick said, looking first at his own baskets, then at the ones on the bike Jut had.

"But nice for bringing things home," Jut reminded him. "You did want Twinkies, didn't you?" Each person in the Howard family got to put one special item a week on the family grocery list. Nick's favorite was Twinkies.

"You don't have to have baskets on your big bike," Jut added. "I don't. Neither does Marty now that's he's got a big bike."

"Can I go in front?" Nick pedaled down the sidewalk in front of Jut.

"Just watch it at Center Street." Jut pedaled slowly and wished he weren't going to the grocery store with his little brother. Talk about boring! At least Miss Brown had had good news about his mother. He was ready for her to be up all the time and for life to return to normal.

When they got inside the grocery store, Jut pulled out their list. "You know what we need," he told Nick. "If you want to help, you can get the stuff on that side of the store and I'll get this side. Here's the list." Jut handed the list to Nick.

"Sure. Meet you at the checkout." Nick wrestled a cart free from the line of carts and set off down the bread and baked goods aisle.

Jut went down the fresh produce aisle. He

put bananas and apples and a bag of oranges in his cart. He added soups, hamburger, eggs, and a bag of sugar. In the prepared foods aisle he picked a few items not on the list. But he knew Marty would like fixing them. He put in a Chinese dinner, a Mexican dinner, and two boxes of macaroni and cheese dinner. He wished Marty could have come because he was sure Marty would have had even better ideas. At the last minute he added a can of tuna fish. Martin-the-chef might learn how to make Jut's favorite: tunafish casserole.

Then he went to the checkout line.

"Guess I'm done too," Nick's voice said behind him. Jut turned around to see an overflowing cart. Nick's dark hair and eyes barely peeked over the mound.

"Woooeee!" Jut exclaimed. He made a rapid count. Three boxes of Twinkies sat on a row of Ring Ding boxes and another row of chocolate cupcake boxes. Root beer and cola bottles lined up neatly across one end of the cart. No space had been wasted. There was a tall pile of ice cream cartons, a pile of Fudgsicle boxes, and a pile of frozen raspberry yogurt bars. The yogurt bars were chocolate coated. Jut couldn't see what was in the middle of the cart, but he thought he could guess.

"We oughta get this stuff home quick," Nick said. "A lot of it's frozen."

Jut walked slowly all around Nick's cart. He didn't want to believe his eyes. Three sacks of potato chips and one of pretzels stuck out the back of the cart. Jut looked at the pretzels a long time before he spoke.

"Where's the bread?" he asked.

"In there," Nick answered confidently. "Somewhere in the middle."

"Somewhere in the middle," Jut repeated. He couldn't think of what to say to Nick. Nick probably thought he'd done a good job.

"Hey! Hurry up!" called the checkout boy. "We close at ten," he added sarcastically.

Jut ignored the checkout. He looked at Nick. "You have to put it back," he said because he couldn't think of any gentle way to say it. "We can't take all that stuff."

"CAN TOO!" Nick shouted hastily, as though he'd been waiting for an argument.

Jut winced. Out of the corner of his eye he saw the manager in a red coat. The manager leaned against the office door and watched.

"Come on, come on," nagged the checkout.

Jut wished he were anywhere but the grocery store and anybody else but Justin Howard. Of course, wishing didn't help. He had to do something and he had to do it *now*.

He leaned down and spoke into Nick's ear. "I don't have the money to pay for all that. It wasn't on our list. If you don't help me put some of it back I will never bring you again. *Anywhere!*" Jut made his voice as threatening as he could. "And this time *I* will be a tattletale and tell Mom. Now help me *put it back*."

"Here's an extra cart," the manager said, pushing an empty cart toward Jut. Gratefully, Jut took the cart and began tossing Nick's goodies into it.

Nick opened his mouth to protest, but Jut put a hand over the opening just in time. "Look, Nick, people're staring at us. You holler and I'll never be your friend again. *I mean it!*"

For a few seconds they were frozen that way, Jut with his hand clamped over Nick's mouth. Then, he took his hand away. "We'll take what we can," he said, "and no more."

"I ain't gonna help," Nick said loudly. He folded his arms at his waist and looked down at the floor.

Jut went on unloading Nick's cart as fast as he could. He burned under all the eyes that were on them, and his mind crackled in anger at Nick. *Okay*, he told himself, *I've had it. This is the brat I went to Back-to-School Night for. Some thanks! Dad can just come home for all I care. This whole idea rots! Running a stupid house all the time. Being a stupid father. Boy, is this DUMB.*

When all of the groceries were paid for and crammed into four bags, Jut turned to leave the store. He didn't care whether Nick came with him or not. He had had it with Nick because Nick was just a spoiled brat.

"Son?"

Jut turned and saw the manager's red coat. He felt himself grow red to match the color of that coat. "Y-yes, sir?" He supposed that the manager would tell him never to come back, to take his troublesome brother and get lost. "I—I, uh," Jut began his painful apology.

"No, no, son. You're the oldest Howard boy, aren't you? Well, I wanted you to know that you handled that real well back there. I can use kids who have self-control. Come to me when you get ready to work." He smiled. "That is, if you like grocery stores as a place to work. And tell your mother that I hope she gets better soon."

Jut blinked in amazement. He couldn't think of anything to say. What a nice person the manager was. The awful red of embarrassment drained out of Jut's face, and he swallowed awkwardly. "Gee, uh, thank you. I guess it'd be all right working in a grocery store . . . as long as I can leave Nick home," he added grimly. He forced a small smile.

The manager put forth a sympathetic hand and they shook hands. "Remember to say howdy at your mom for me. She *is* getting better, isn't she?"

"Yes, sir, but she can't do it fast enough to suit me!"

"You have your hands full," the manager agreed as he headed on back to his office. "See you around."

Jut pushed the cart outside and loaded the four grocery bags into the four bike baskets. Nick came over to him as he stuffed the last bag down into its basket.

"I'm sorry," Nick said. His voice wobbled.

Jut listened in stony silence. *He sure as heck ought to be sorry,* he thought. *Whole store watched us. See if I ever go anyplace with him again.*

"I'm really, really sorry, Jut," Nick said again. His voice wobbled even more than on the first apology.

Jut looked out of the corner of his eye and saw that Nick was ready to cry. *Good,* thought Jut, who knew how Nick hated to cry because it was baby. If Nick cried for ten hours, Jut would be glad. His face set, Jut continued to ignore Nick. He got on his bike and headed out of the parking lot. Nick could come if he wanted to. Jut didn't care.

Of course, Nick followed Jut closely. After one block of the punishing silence, Nick called out to Jut. "What's a guy sposeta do? Throw himself in front of a truck? I *said* I was *sorry.*"

Jut could tell, without turning around, that Nick was crying. But now, instead of being glad at Nick's tears, Jut was sorry. He was sorry the whole thing had happened. Nick was right. He had apologized. And it was over now.

"Yeah," Jut said. He looked straight ahead. Nick wouldn't want Jut to see him in tears. "That was good stuff you picked. Probably, when Dad gets home, we can afford more of that stuff. If Mom lets us have it."

"She won't," Nick snuffled, knowing his mother.

"I'm afraid you're right," Jut answered. He pedaled his bike slowly and steered carefully, hoping to get the eggs home without breaking them. "Heard any good songs lately?"

"Yeah, a brand-new one!" Nick's voice was bright again.

"Let's have it." Jut braced himself.

Nick took a big breath. *"Great big globs of greasy, grimy gopher guts,*

Mutilated monkey meat,
Chopped-up baby parakeet.
All wrapped up in itty, bitty birdy feet,
Yum, yum, don't forget to lick the spoon."

Jut laughed. "Great song for before dinner, Nick. Gus will love it."

"Wanta sing with me?"

8

Gus's Fissy

"Martin, that was just yummy." Mrs. Howard got up from the table.

Marty beamed with pleasure. There had been many compliments about the Mexican dinner he had fixed.

Briefly, Jut was annoyed. Why was food so special? Nobody had said how nice it was to have *clean clothes* after he had done the washing. Washing was a lot more work than dinner out of a box, for cripes sake.

"And now it's nighty-night for Mother. Can you believe it?"

"No, I can't," Jut said. "It's only seven

o'clock. How can you sleep so much?"

"But I was up two hours this afternoon. And two this morning. That's progress." She turned to Marty. "What's for dinner tomorrow night, O Chef?"

"I think. . . ." Marty cleaned his glasses on his sweatshirt while he thought. "I think we'll have hamburgers. I've got a big science project due Monday, and I can't *live* in the kitchen!"

"I understand," grinned Mrs. Howard. "Gus is finished with dinner. I'll put him on the couch in the living room with his books and maybe he'll stay out of your hair for a while." She and Gus left the kitchen.

"Isn't it time Dad called again?" Marty asked Jut as they began clearing the table.

"Yeah," chimed Nick. "I didn't get to talk to him last time." Nick took his yo-yo out of his pocket and began practicing Around the World.

"Take it to your room, Nick," Jut said when the yo-yo crashed into a picture on the wall.

"Dad'll probably call this weekend." Jut began loading plates into the dishwasher. "Why, Marty?"

"Mom said she'd ask Dad if we could go hunting even if he isn't here. He promised this was my year, remember? Ten. Just like for you."

"TB! TB!" Gus pulled at Jut's jeans pocket to get his attention.

"No, Gus. Not now. Ask Nick to fix TV for you." Jut picked Gus up, faced him toward the living room, and gave him a little push in that direction.

Gus left the kitchen and looked for Nick. No Nick. While Jut and Marty talked about hunting season, Gus was on his own. He had to amuse himself. For a while, he fiddled with the television knobs, trying to get a picture. He pulled and pushed several knobs, and just as something looked like it would be a picture, it disappeared. Gus waited a long time, but no picture came on the screen.

He sat in his small rocking chair in front of the blank screen and rocked back and forth. That was boring too, just like the TV.

Gus pushed his chair over to the television where the goldfish bowl sat on top. He climbed up and peered down into the stale, dirty water. Marty had not cleaned the bowl

65

or fed his fish in days. The fish were preparing for death. Four starving fish swam in funereal circles while Gus watched.

"Fissy . . . fissy," crooned Gus, one finger in the water. He touched one fish and it didn't dart away from his finger like it usually did. In fact, the fish seemed to lean into his finger. Gus put his hand in the bowl and lifted out the fish that had been so friendly. The goldfish lay in Gus's hand and gasped weakly. Gently, Gus stroked it. "Nice fissy . . . nice fissy."

Because it seemed like a good idea, Gus put the goldfish on his tongue. He stuck his tongue way out and the goldfish fit perfectly. Gus peered cross-eyed over his nose down at the fish.

He closed his mouth slowly and the fish stayed in place, entombed in Gus's mouth. He opened his mouth and stuck his tongue out. There it was again. Right in place. Gus opened and closed his mouth several times, moving his tongue in and out—giving the goldfish rides.

"Goood fissy," Gus said. Except that when he said "fissy," he swallowed. The goldfish slid

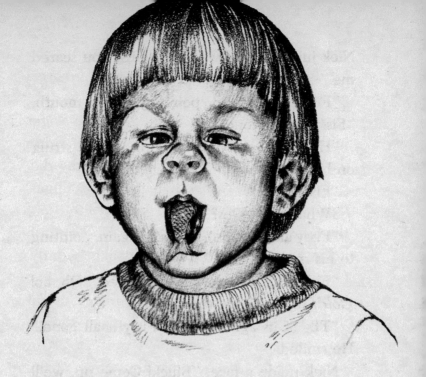

down his throat into its final tomb: a human
stomach. Gus stuck his tongue way out. *No
fissy*.

"Fissy aaall gone," Gus said sadly. He wan-
dered out of the living room and up the stairs
toward the room he shared with Nick. Gus
checked each room upstairs until he came to
his and Nick's room.

Nick, busy with his yo-yo, didn't even see
Gus come in. When Gus pulled on Nick's shirt,

Nick jumped. "Yow! Oh, hi, Gus. You scared me."

"Fissy," Gus said, pointing to his mouth. "Fissy aaaall gone."

"Huh?" asked Nick, winding up the string on his yo-yo.

"Fissy."

"What fishy, Gus?"

"Fissy aaaall gone," Gus said again, pointing to his mouth.

"Fishy?" Nick's dark eyes blinked. "Oh, no! *Goldfish*, Gus? On the TV?"

"TB," Gus agreed. "TB. Fissy aaall gone." He smiled.

Nick made a face. "Bluck! Come on, we'll go tell Jut and Marty."

As soon as Nick and Gus got to the kitchen, Gus said, "Aaaaall gone fissy."

"Gus ate a goldfish." Nick looked from Marty to Jut. "It's true. I checked. One's gone and the bowl stinks."

Marty groaned loudly. "RATS!" His fist pounded the counter.

"You said you were going to CLEAN THE BOWL!" Jut shouted. "You told me you were going to take care of it! I can't DO EVERY-THING!"

Marty glared at Jut. "Yeah, yeah! Don't tell me your troubles! I came in, just like I said, all ready to clean the bowl—and the stupid phone rang. Then the doctor came. And I had Gus and dinner to fix and all YOU had to do was get a few LOUSY GROCERIES!"

"You guys're yelling," Nick said. "You're gonna wake Mom."

Jut shut his mouth on words he was dying to say. He glared around the room, daring anyone to speak.

"Fissy aaall gone," Gus repeated softly.

"Okay, okay!" Marty left the kitchen. When he came back he said, "Yup. One of 'em's gone, all right." He looked down at Gus. "How could you put something like that in your *mouth*?" He shuddered.

"Gus'll eat *anything*," Jut said. "I'd better call the doctor. We don't want him to get sick." The idea of one more sick person was so awful Jut didn't even want to think about it.

"We eat fish all the time," Marty observed.

"Cooked, but what's the difference?"

"Ours are cleaner," Nick answered.

"You stay out of it!" Marty glowered at Nick.

"Shut up, you guys, so I can hear the doctor." Jut called the doctor at his home, which was only three blocks away. "Maybe fish is fish," he said to Marty, "but we have to *know*. It should *never have happened*," he added darkly, frowning at Marty.

Jut talked first and the doctor listened. Then Jut listened while Dr. Collins talked. At last Jut said, "Okay, and thanks a lot. I don't think Mom needs to know about this, do you?" He thanked the doctor again and hung up.

"You were right, Marty. The fish'll digest just like other fish, the doctor says. He said nobody should eat another fish though, just to keep Gus company." Jut smiled, relieved.

Marty let out a big puff of air. "Whew! I'll get the bowl and clean it. Maybe we ought to put it up where Gus can't get it."

"On the mantel over the fireplace," Jut called after him. He looked down at Gus, then, who seemed to be okay even if he had eaten a slimy goldfish. Probably other people had eaten goldfish—on a dare maybe, or to get into some kind of club. Jut reached for his book of records.

"Hey, Marty! My book says somebody ate three hundred live goldfish once. Bleccch!"

Marty came through the kitchen doorway. He held his fishbowl way out in front of him. "Pukey in there. I don't think this is the reason, either. What else could stink in the living room?"

9

Time Out

"Have a good time!" Mrs. Howard leaned against the front door jamb and waved good-bye.

Jut, his brothers, and Amazon Brown waved back. Gus had been strapped into the front seat of the car between the nurse and Jut. Marty and Nick sat in the back seat.

"I smelled that smell again," Miss Brown said, backing out of the driveway. "It isn't worse, but it isn't gone, either. Can't your mom smell it?"

"Where're we going?" Nick leaned forward.

"It's a surprise. You'll know when we get

there," the nurse told Nick. "Couldn't you guys get rid of the smell?"

"Well," Jut began uncomfortably, "we haven't tried yet. Not really."

"We thought it was my fish. Only it wasn't." Marty hesitated. "I went in there last night, when everybody'd gone to bed, just to smell around. Didn't find a thing, except the smell."

In the front seat, Jut grinned. "That's funny. I did the same thing. Lucky we didn't bump into each other."

Miss Brown steered the car up a ramp leading onto the freeway. Above the freeway, the sign said CINCINNATI in big letters. "Has your mom said anything about the smell?" she persisted.

"No. She probably doesn't want us to feel like we're not doing a good job," Jut said slowly. But that was how he felt every time he thought about the odor. For a couple of days he had tried *not* to think about it at all. "We have to clean this weekend," he decided out loud. "All day tomorrow. That'll fix it."

Marty groaned, and Nick said, "Not me, boy."

73

Nurse Brown jumped into the conversation, changing the subject. She asked Jut to tell her about the junior high basketball team, about the coach, and about tryouts. She promised to save plenty of time to work with Jut before tryouts. Everyone but Gus talked about sports the rest of the trip.

It was Marty who guessed where they were going. "Doesn't this road go right by Riverfront Stadium?" he asked, hope alive in his voice.

"You betchum." Amazon Brown grinned. "Give that boy a silver dollar."

"*Really?*" Jut couldn't believe it. "But it's the World Series. We'll never get in."

"Wanta bet?" the nurse teased.

No one bet. She was too sure of herself. "We have ticket pools at the hospital where I work part-time," she explained. "I won four tickets to this game. Didn't know what I was going to do with them for sure, till I met you guys. Great secret, huh?" She looked very pleased with herself.

Nick was busy counting people and seats. "Who's gonna hold Gus?" he asked.

"Geez, Nick!" Marty scolded. "It's just lucky

we get to go. Who cares who holds Gus! He doesn't have *any manners at all,*" he said, leaning forward to talk directly to Miss Brown.

"I do, too!" Nick kicked Marty in the leg.

"Look, you guys," the nurse said loudly, "if you fight you're going to ruin my day. I like every one of you just the way you are. That's why I'm happy about our being together, okay? Now no more arguing. Jut, pull that map out of my jacket pocket and see if you can help me find a good place to park. Within three miles of our seats—ha, ha."

Jut watched later as Miss Brown handed four tickets to a gatekeeper. He felt as if he were in a funny kind of dream. He'd always wanted to see a World Series game. He had watched the Series every year on television, and this year his favorite Ohio team, the Cincinnati Reds, had made it. He hadn't been able to pay much attention to the pennant race, though, because running the house had taken so much time.

But now he was here. For real. First game of the World Series! He sniffed the special ballpark smells and crunched old popcorn under his feet. A girl selling pennants walked by and a man hawking ice-cold beer. The spicy, fat hot dogs advertised themselves with a fragrance Jut couldn't resist. "How about if I buy everybody a hot dog?" he offered, reaching for his wallet.

Nurse Brown laughed. "Your mom sent enough lunch money for us to camp out here for a week. Do you want to get the whole lunch now, on our way to our seats?"

"Num, num," Gus said. He patted Nurse Brown's cheek. "Gus num num."

Loaded with lunch, everybody proceeded to their seats behind third base. "Great, great seats," Marty said with gratitude, his mouth full of hot dog and mustard.

For a while, then, nobody said anything. They looked around the stadium, watched the pitchers warming up in the bullpen, and ate. A pop man walked by their row and Nurse Brown bought five more cans of pop—creme soda this time, something they all liked, but hardly ever had.

Halfway through the creme soda, the ballgame got underway with cheering heavy all over the stadium. Half of Cincinnati had turned out to see her beloved Reds fight and win the pennant. Then the Reds beat Philadelphia three straight in the playoffs. Now, they were playing the first game of the seven-game series against the New York Yankees.

"We'd better win today," Jut told Amazon Brown. "It'd be a great psychological thing, don't you think?"

"I haffa peepee," Gus said, his face distressed.

"Oh, dear." Miss Brown immediately set Gus on the cement floor in front of her. "Did anybody see where the toilets were as we came in?"

"Yup. I have to go, too, so I'll take him," Marty offered. "The toilets aren't far away. We'll be right back." He grabbed Gus's hand and off they went.

"Their pitcher is good," the nurse observed. She had brought along a pair of binoculars and passed them to Jut. "Watch his form. He throws so naturally you'd think he'd been born with that ball in his hand."

Jut nodded in gloomy agreement as he peered through the binoculars. "They've got more in the bullpen, just as good. That's what'll kill us. They're hard to hit."

The first inning went swiftly, with Cincinnati scoring a run. The stands grew even noisier, if such a thing were possible. Halfway through the second inning, after the Yanks scored, Nurse Brown said, "Do you think we should be worried about Marty and Gus?"

"No. Marty's probably letting Gus walk around some so he'll be ready to sit again when they come back. Gus doesn't like to sit very much."

The second inning ended, with the score tied 1–1. "I'm hungry," Nick said. He looked down into his empty box of Cracker Jacks.

"Here, have an apple," Miss Brown offered. "I brought lots." She looked at Jut. "I am getting nervous about Marty and Gus."

"Me, too," Jut agreed. The relief on his face was great as he looked behind him and saw Marty approaching their row of seats.

"Hey!" Jut said sharply. "Where's Gus?"

"Well," Marty began slowly. He leaned

against Jut's aisle seat. "He's sorta lost . . . I think."

Nurse Brown's eyes grew enormous and her face paled. *"Sorta lost?"* she repeated in a strangled voice. "You can't be *sorta lost.* You either *are* or you *aren't!*" She stood up and ran a shaking hand through her hair. "Quick, Marty, where did you see him last?"

"In the john," Marty replied. "He wanted to go in and be by himself. So I put him in a stall. He likes it to be private," he explained to the nurse.

"Yes, yes, hurry up and tell me!"

"I put him in the stall, and I went over to use a . . . a . . . , well, you know." Marty was clearly embarrassed to be discussing bathroom arrangements with a woman who wasn't part of their family. "A urinal," he said finally.

"And? For God's sake, Marty, hurry up!"

"And when I turned around, his stall was open, and he wasn't there anymore! He can't have gone very far. I looked all over the john, and out in the hallway, but I couldn't find him. I thought I'd better tell you guys so we could all look."

Jut had been silent all this time. Now he tore his eyes away from the ballgame and stood up like the nurse. "I'll take Nick with me. Spread out, okay? Ask people if they've seen him. We'll meet in front of the men's john in fifteen minutes." He looked at his watch. "That's two-thirty. If we haven't found him by then, we'll have the PA system announce that he's lost."

Nurse Brown nodded mechanically. "Right. Good idea, Jut. Let's hurry up, everybody." Her face was still very pale and her hands were clenched by her sides.

Jut and Nick, Marty, and the nurse fanned out to hunt for Gus. They called Gus's name, asked strangers if they'd seen a two-year-old in navy corduroy coveralls, and grew more upset as the minutes went by.

At two-thirty, when they met in front of the men's toilet, there was still no Gus. "He's lost," Nick announced to no one in particular.

"Of course he's lost!" snapped Miss Brown. "Oh, I'm sorry, Nick. It's not your fault. I'm going to the public address room this minute and have it announced that he's missing." She sounded as if she might burst into tears any second.

"I'll take Nick and Marty back to our seats," Jut said. "He's probably okay. Mom said he had walked away from her in stores a couple times and was always all right. Don't worry too much." Jut spoke firmly to cheer the over-wrought nurse.

He and his brothers heard the announcement about Gus as soon as they reached their seats. A hush fell over Riverfront Stadium as the announcement was made two times in a row. Gus was described very carefully to the thousands of people who would now be able to help in the search. Like most announcements about missing children, it brought quick success.

"Look at the scoreboard!" Nick squealed, pointing.

Marty and Jut read the words on the lighted scoreboard: "GUS IS FOUND. LET'S HEAR IT FOR GUS!"

Another kind of roar rippled through the stadium, this time a roar of laughter. Large groups of friendly people cheered, "Yay, Gus!

Yay, Gus!"

Nick frowned around at the cheering crowds. "Big deal. You'd think he'd done something real cool, 'stead of getting himself lost. Bet if *I* got lost, all *I'd* get is a spanking."

Jut understood. "You were a baby, too, you know. If you'd been lost, we'd have been just as scared. Want another hot dog?"

"Here we are," Amazon Brown said as she and Gus joined the boys in their row. "From now on, he goes nowhere without *me*!" She settled Gus in her lap. "Want to know where he was?" she asked, her breathing rapid. Jut could tell she was still terribly upset.

"He was eating an ice cream cone in the ice cream stand on the *other side* of the stadium. Don't ask me how he got there. But *he* wasn't worried at all. Calm as gosh."

Jut nodded sympathetically. "That's what Mom said, remember? Marty used to do the same thing. I guess we don't get upset since it's sort of a family habit."

"Well, not *today* it isn't." She took the belt off her jacket and tied it around Gus's waist. The other end she tied around her knee.

"Okay, champ. We're joined for life."

"I'd rather have ice cream than a hot dog, Jut," Nick said. "I'm hungry."

"That kid is fooling, isn't he?" The nurse looked at Jut.

"No. Nick's not as interested in the game as we are."

"Game? What game?" Miss Brown joked. "Ye gods, would you look at that! While we weren't watching, we scored two more runs, and the Yanks didn't score any. We're ahead! We have to get busy and yell for the good guys to score some more!"

The rest of the game went more smoothly for the Howards. Gus was never farther than a jacket belt away from Nurse Brown, and after the seventh-inning stretch, when the Reds scored twice, he fell asleep in her lap.

"You guys yell for me," she whispered over the baby's sleeping head. "It'd be wonderful if he took a nap."

All of the Howards yelled in a thorough way, and the result was that Cincinnati won, 5–1. Jut couldn't remember when he'd seen a better game.

"I don't know how to thank you," he told the nurse on the drive home. "It's the best sports event we ever saw. Dad'll be green with envy."

"When does your dad come home?" the nurse asked.

"Maybe three or four weeks, maybe only two. He says it depends."

"Well, we'll do something together another Saturday. This was fun—in spite of Gus's scaring the wits out of me."

"You know," Nick said thoughtfully, "my stomach hurts."

10

Man the Mops

"I don't care if nobody wants to," Jut said with authority. "We have to. The whole room stinks." Behind him, another pan clunked onto the kitchen floor. Gus was playing in the pan cupboard again. Mrs. Thomas didn't baby-sit on weekends.

Hands clenched into fists, Jut looked first at Marty, then Nick. "Look, I don't want to clean either! But if we work this morning, we can play this afternoon."

"Okay, okay," Marty sighed, as he yanked open the broom closet door. "Dirt doesn't bother me," he muttered. "I never even see it."

"Me, too," said Nick.

"Me, too," Jut agreed. "But smells bother me. And we're going to get rid of ours before Mom says something." Jut was getting angry at that stupid smell.

"I'll vacuum," Nick offered suddenly. "I like to push the vacuum."

"Great, Nick. Let's take everything in there and get it over with." Jut pulled rags and cleaning bottles out of the broom closet.

Nick and the vacuum roared out of the kitchen.

While Nick pushed the vacuum around the living room, Jut wiped things with a dustrag. He kept sniffing as he went. One side of the room was much worse, he decided. He stopped dusting and stood back to look at the fireplace wall in the living room. That's where the smell was strongest.

"What's the matter?" Marty yelled over the vacuum motor.

Jut pointed to the massive old fireplace. He held his nose with two fingers and pointed with the other hand.

Marty stopped looking under chair and sofa cushions and came to stand next to Jut.

"Go smell around the fireplace," Jut said in Marty's ear. Marty smelled the entire fireplace wall and came back to stand next to Jut again.

"That's it," Marty agreed. He and Jut just stood and looked at the fireplace.

Of all the special things in the Howards' old house, the fireplace was the best. It had been Mrs. Howard's reason for choosing the house years ago. She said it was the most handsome fireplace in all of Ohio. It was tall enough inside that Marty could stand in it and his head didn't touch the top. Its mantel was hand-carved, solid oak.

To the left of the fireplace opening was an oak panel that ran from floor to ceiling. On the right was an identical oak panel. However, on the right, below mantel height, was a wood cupboard. The knob on the wood cupboard door had been carved by hand like the mantel.

"Probably in the wood cupboard," Jut said. He looked around with relief as the vacuum sound moved into the front hall. "How about the wood cupboard?" he said again, in case Marty hadn't heard.

"Sure. Don't know why we didn't think of

it before." Marty went into the cupboard, nose sniffing loudly. He sniffed each pile of wood stacked inside. Slowly, then, he backed out and closed the door with the wooden knob. "Not there. Just smells like wood. If you want the truth, it smells *better* in there than it does out here."

That wasn't a truth that Jut wanted. He paced up and down in front of the fireplace and continued to sniff every few seconds. "I just *don't get it.*"

"Still stinks, huh?" asked Nick. He was pushing the vacuum, but he had turned it off.

"Yes, it stinks!" Marty snapped.

Nick's dark eyes were bright. "Maybe Gus went in the planter again," he suggested. Everyone in the family remembered the early days of Gus's toilet training when he had made a mistake in the rhododendron planter by the front window.

"Nope," Jut said. "I already checked that."

"Maybe Pierpont went behind the couch," Nick said.

Marty shook his head no. "I looked for that. He didn't. There is *no reason* for this room to smell."

88

"Wrong," Jut said with a forced smile. "There's a reason. We just can't find it." The smile, put on to cheer people up, faded away. He tried to tell himself that it wasn't his fault that the living room smelled, but he didn't believe himself. He was in charge. And the living room stunk. Those were the facts.

"Miaaaow?" Eleanore came through the doorway into the living room. She sat down and looked at Jut and Marty.

"You're right, Jut. She sure isn't any thinner." Marty's voice was doleful.

At the sound of his voice, Eleanore got to her feet and walked over to be petted. She rubbed her tail against Marty's leg and sat down facing the fireplace, her back to the room. Marty scratched her head and thought out loud.

"Look at the fireplace, Jut. See anything funny?"

Jut looked. "I see Eleanore. That's funny. She hasn't been in here with us for ages."

"But *we* haven't been in here," Nick said, "because it's stinky."

"Has *she* been in here?"

"Yeah. I see her in here sometimes, real

early in the morning before you guys're up."

"Really? You aren't making that up?" Marty's tone was skeptical.

Nick bristled. "You callin' me a liar?" he began.

"No one is *lying*," Jut said before a fight got started. He turned back to Marty. "You know, it's a *rotten* smell. *Garbagy*, just like the nurse said. Terrible."

"See anything funny about the fireplace?" Marty asked again. His hand slid down Eleanore's tail as she rose, stretched, and walked back into the kitchen. *"Well?"* Marty persisted.

"It's not the same," Jut said, his head tipped to one side. "There's two of everything in this house, but not two wood cupboards. Is that what you mean?" Jut wondered why they hadn't thought about that. The house had everything in pairs. Two windows, or four windows, and so on. In the dining room were two old wall sconces and two chandeliers. Mr. Howard called it the Noah Syndrome.

"I'll get the phone," Nick said.

"Mom said she'd get the phone while we cleaned. But put away the vacuum, Nick." Jut could hardly think about normal things. He had an idea that was so exciting . . .

"Martin?" Mrs. Howard's voice came down the stairway. "Get on the phone in the kitchen. You can ask your father about hunting. Jut, you talk next, and be sure to let Nick talk, too."

All of them raced into the kitchen. "Hey, Dad, I'm ten this fall, remember?" Marty said across the miles to Europe. "Jut and I want to go hunting, and I'll be careful—just like you showed me. *Please!*"

Jut watched Marty's face as he listened. "Well?" he whispered, not reading an answer on Marty's face.

"He 'n' Mom are arguing," Marty whispered back. "But I think it's gonna be all right."

A few minutes later, Marty nodded happily into the telephone. "Yup! Just like you say. I *promise*. Thanks a lot, Dad. Here's Jut."

Jut talked with his father for several minutes. He learned that the only hunting would be on a friend's farm outside of town. That way, an adult, Mr. Howard's friend, would be there all the time.

"That's great, Dad. His farm has hundreds

of squirrels. And, Dad, I've got a question about our house? How old is it?" Jut held his breath. He listened, then asked, "How about the library? Wouldn't it be in a book somewhere?"

When Jut finished talking, Nick talked. "Dad's coming home pretty soon," Nick said when he was through. "Maybe only two weeks. Mom said it was her turn to talk now."

"What's this about the house?" Marty asked.

"I'll tell you later, when I've had a chance to check," Jut told him. "Probably nothing. Let's put away this cleaning stuff. We can give Gus a sandwich and put him to bed for a nap so we can play ball."

That night, when everyone was asleep, Jut tiptoed downstairs to the living room. A violent odor of pine greeted him. Marty had covered up the bad smell with a good smell: pine forest. Jut was struck by the power of the canned forest. *I don't know which is worse*, he thought.

Quietly, he made his way in the dark toward the fireplace wall. As he put a hand forward to the left oak panel, he heard something. Just a little something. But something.

Jut swallowed and pulled his hand back from the wall. Both arms grew rigid at his sides as he listened. He felt his bare feet turn to ice and he needed to go to the bathroom. Was the something a some*one*? Another tiny sound reached Jut's ears. Then a small, warm foot stepped on his foot.

"Miaow?"

"Cripes!" Jut exploded. "Eleanore! What're you doing in here at night?"

"Miaaaow," she returned. She sat down next to Jut's leg.

He bent over to pet the cat. "You're getting weirder and weirder, Eleanore," Jut accused her. "Now go upstairs with Mom where you belong." He set the cat on her feet and pushed her toward the hallway and its steps to the second floor. "Go on."

Eleanore walked a few steps and sat down. Even in the dark she managed to look stubborn. Jut got the feeling she would go only when she was good and ready. Disgruntled, he turned back to the reason for being in the living room at midnight.

Again, his hand reached out for the fireplace

wall. He felt along the mantelpiece until he came to the left side of the fireplace. He felt up and down the smooth oak panel. Just like the other side, he thought, but no cupboard. No little round knob. Just a smooth panel. Maybe.

Jut pulled his hand away from the smoothness of the panel. He made his hand into a fist. And knocked. Thump, thump, thump. Persistently, Jut knocked on the oak panel. Thump. Move over. Thump. Thump.

And then he heard it. Below the level of the mantel the *thump, thump* became *thunk, thunk*. A looser, lighter, less responsible sound altogether. A hollow sound.

"And it isn't a wood cupboard, bet anything," Jut said aloud.

"Miaooow," agreed Eleanore.

11

Marty the Hunter

Jut spent hours the next week thinking about their house and the newly discovered panel and its secret. Was the panel hiding a space or not? If so, how *big* a space? Marty, fascinated by the discovery, thumped and thunked on the oak panel, enjoying the hollow sound below mantel level.

"Odd we didn't think of it before," Mrs. Howard said, "since everything else in this house is in pairs." She called the Hampshire librarian and asked that a book be sent out from the county library.

"The book will tell us," she assured Jut after dinner one evening. "The librarian said that every old house in Red Oak County is in that book. I always meant to learn our house's history. It's fun to be actually doing it."

"This time it's 'Spring Wildflowers,'" Marty announced, coming into the kitchen. He pitched an empty spray can into the garbage bag under the sink. "Very powerful stuff. Covers up the smell completely."

Jut and his mother groaned together. "For whatever *that's* worth," Jut joked.

"Well, we're going to *find the smell.*" Marty's tone was confident. "Did you find Dad's hunting vest, Mom? He said I could wear it."

Marty could think of nothing except the opening day of hunting. Jut could only think about the house and the awful smell he couldn't get rid of. It was a long week. Finally, it was Saturday morning and the opening day of hunting season.

"You boys're doing fine," Mr. Plattner told them. "Four squirrels in the first hour is good. Squirrels're smart little buggers."

"It's my fourth season, Mr. Plattner." Jut held up four fingers. "I'll be thirteen in a couple weeks."

The farmer grinned. "Your dad wrote; said you'd be an old pro. Said I could turn you loose after a bit. How about if we hunt together until dinner at noon? Then, after dinner, you can hunt the creek and woods without me."

Marty's eyes shone behind his glasses. "I need to talk to Mrs. Plattner about how to fix squirrel. I've never cooked it."

"Marty's our cook," Jut explained to his father's friend. He went on to explain how his mother was sick and they were keeping it a secret so his dad wouldn't come home. "We always eat what we hunt," Jut finished. He wanted Mr. Plattner to know that the Howards were honorable hunters. "Our favorite is pheasant, but squirrels are good, so they're second."

"Let's sit under this hickory," suggested Mr. Plattner. He lowered himself to the ground at the foot of the tree. "Lots of squirrels around here last week."

"That was *last* week," joked Marty.

"Ssh," warned Jut. "Think squirrels're deaf?"

The three sat in friendly silence and waited

for the first foolhardy squirrel to move. The longer they were quiet, the braver the squirrels would get. Eventually, one of them would decide that danger had passed. That would be his last—and worst—decision.

"You say you've got too many squirrels?" Jut whispered to Mr. Plattner. A strange thought had crossed his mind in all the quietness. What if they shot *all* the squirrels? A woods without squirrels would be unnatural, wrong somehow.

"Got too many by about two, three hundred! They got into my feed corn last winter." Mr. Plattner shook his head with disgust.

Jut nodded. That was different, then. They were ridding the farm of a pest. A few killed would certainly not endanger all squirrels in southern Ohio. And they would eat them, of course.

The friendly silence resumed. As though they were in on the plot, the squirrels also kept quiet. Perhaps the earlier shots had alarmed them. Jut could still hear the gun's sharp crack in his mind if he thought about it.

Nine o'clock became ten, then eleven, then

eleven-thirty. They had sat under the hickory, two oaks, and a chestnut by that time. Just as they were ready to go to the farmhouse for dinner, Mr. Plattner and Jut each got a squirrel. "At this rate," the farmer grinned, "I'd better rent a giant safe-deposit box for that corn next winter!"

"We'll get lots after lunch," Marty assured him.

"This is no *lunch*," Mr. Plattner said, swiftly skinning his squirrel. He took Jut's squirrel and made a quick slit under its tail. He stood on the tail then and pulled the pelt down to the head. A rapid slice, and the headless squirrel joined the other in a plastic bag. "Here, Jut," the farmer said, giving him the bag. "Anybody hungry?"

Not very, Jut thought, mindful of the headless squirrels. The words to Nick's song about greasy, grimy gopher guts ran through his mind. Out loud he said, "I'll bet Mrs. Plattner is a really good cook."

Mrs. Plattner was an excellent cook. One look at her table and Jut's appetite returned. He and Marty ate until they felt sick. Then they had a piece of pie and a piece of cake.

If they didn't try her desserts, Mrs. Plattner said, she was going to be insulted.

Jut forced down the last bite of cake and wondered if she would also be insulted if he threw up. He looked at Marty and could tell Marty felt the same way he did.

Mr. Plattner told them to be "damn careful," and lay down on the living room couch for a nap. Jut and Marty thanked Mrs. Plattner and walked slowly away from the house toward the creek.

"One more bite . . . ," Jut said carefully. He walked carefully, too. He was afraid to do anything suddenly because it might make him barf.

Marty, too, was moving with care. "When kids say they're full, why don't people believe them?"

"Probably parents would," Jut observed, "but the Plattners just have cows and chickens."

"And squirrels." Marty walked faster. "Getting late. It's after one already."

"I promised Mom we'd be home by five because she's paying a sitter a fortune she said."

"We need a couple more squirrels," Marty said. He and Jut crouched under a tall oak next to the Plattners' creek.

After about an hour, Jut coughed. "I think this is dull—"

"Ssssh!" Marty's voice was tense. "Get ready. Over there," he hissed, jerking his head toward a tree across the creek.

Jut saw three squirrels scooting out onto a long branch—chittering, scolding, ignoring the boys across the creek.

"Quick!" Marty breathed. Two shots rang out at once. "Now," Marty exulted, "we can have a real squirrel feed, just as if Dad was home."

"Even if we don't get any more," Marty said again while they cleaned the squirrels, "this is just right for a meal. Or . . . we could wait till Dad got home and *then* eat 'em. Freeze 'em now."

"Great idea, the freezing," Jut said hastily. He pushed down his feeling of distaste as they cleaned the squirrels. He hadn't felt this way last year.

When they had stowed the cleaned squirrels and settled down the creek under a different tree, Jut spoke. "Don't you think we've got enough?"

"Nope. Every meal we can freeze is worth something. Besides, the first day you went hunting you got seven. I've only got five so far."

Jut sighed. He could see that Marty would use any excuse he could think of to stay on the farm and hunt. Of course, he was enjoying it, and had proved to be a good shot, too.

The silence by the creek was almost total. For a time, nothing moved except an occasional leaf on its autumn trip to the ground. Then birds began visiting with one another again and invisible animals made their usual noises. Jut's nose itched, and his left foot went to sleep. He yawned three times and decided he had to stand up.

"Don't move," warned Marty, seeing Jut begin to unfold. "We're gonna get those crows over there."

"*Crows?*"

"Farmers *hate* crows!" Marty hissed. "Didn't you hear Mrs. Plattner at lunch, griping about her garden and the crows? Get ready, Jut."

Both boys raised their guns in slow motion until the butt of each rested against a shoulder. Two swift cracks sounded almost in unison and two crows were finished.

Jut went toward the crows while Marty ejected the used cartridges from both guns. Jut didn't know what he'd do with the crows, but he couldn't leave them lying there like that. Even if they were a terrible farm pest.

As he reached down to pick them up, he first thought, then said aloud to Marty, "I don't like this anymore. I don't know why. I just don't." He picked up one crow. "Put this with your squirrels. I don't have any more room." Only then did he realize that he had already put one of the crows into a pocket of his hunting vest. Automatically.

"Huh?"

"We eat what we hunt." Jut's face was set. "We'll take them home."

Marty didn't say anything. He put the crow into a pocket of his dad's hunting vest.

Jut and Marty thanked the Plattners. It was late, Jut told them, and they had to get back since they'd promised their mother. Mrs.

Plattner pushed a sack into Jut's hands.

"This is the rest of the pie. And half that cake. Tell your mother I hope she's better soon. And, Marty, remember to cook those squirrels long and slow, with onions."

Everybody said thank you and good-bye again. Marty hurried after Jut, who was setting a fast pace. Five o'clock was coming. Marty nearly had to run to keep up with Jut's longer legs. He started a conversation several times, but Jut's answers were brief. Finally, he said, "Hey! You mad at me or something?"

Jut slowed down. "No. Of course not. It's not your fault. Hunting's okay for you, I think." There was an awkward pause. "But I don't like it anymore, and I'm not real sure *why*."

"That's okay!" Marty's voice was loud. "Nobody *has* to like hunting. I just like *everything* to do with animals, and bugs, and outdoors. But that's *me*."

"I-I *used* to like it," Jut said, almost as if he were talking to himself. He turned to look at Marty, who had tried to make him feel all right about not liking hunting.

"But now you *don't* like it." Marty's tone

was matter-of-fact. "Maybe after *I've* hunted a few years *I* won't like it either. That's life." He shrugged his shoulders.

Jut heard what Marty meant, and felt better. Marty was a good brother—lots smarter than some kids he knew who were ten. Jut hadn't ever been good friends with Marty, until lately. Of course, a brother wasn't like a father.

Jut walked faster again. He wanted his father. They needed to talk about this, only his father was far away.

12

Birds and Vegetables

"Can Gus stay in the house with you for a while? Nick wants to help us clean the birds. Out in the shed."

"Birds? I thought you'd gotten only squirrels. And we put them in the freezer last night."

"Got a couple birds, too," Jut said vaguely, waving his mother out of the kitchen. "So we'll fix dinner this afternoon while you sleep. Just watch Gus for a little while, okay? Then he can be in the kitchen with us."

Jut changed into old clothes and joined Marty and Nick in the toolshed where the mower, tools, and old bike parts lived. And where the two dead crows waited. They hung down from the ceiling by string. Each separate. Each being aged. Marty had insisted that they be aged for one day.

Jut had told him he was crazy, but Marty had been firm. He would do it, he had said. Jut had been glad to let Marty do it.

"Well, let's get started." Jut could look at the birds today and not care very much. And now they would be eaten, just like all game should be eaten.

"Right," said Marty. He cut the crows down and put them on the toolbench. He held the knife and looked puzzled. "How can you tell where to cut?"

"Ccccckkkkkk," Nick said, making a slicing gesture across his neck.

"Not yet," Jut told him. "I think you're supposed to hold them by the head and dunk them in boiling water. Then, we should pluck the feathers. Like duck, Marty, remember?"

"Oh, yeah. I remember this job stinks." Marty frowned.

"So do those birds." Nick had backed toward the shed door.

"They do not!" Marty put a hand protectively over one of the crows.

The entire time Marty and Jut worked to clean the crows, Nick said that they stunk. Jut could tell that Nick was feeling left out again. Marty argued with Nick. "Look at that!" Marty said to Nick when the birds were plucked and cut into cooking-size pieces. "Looks almost like a pheasant breast."

"Hah!" snorted Nick.

Jut laughed. "Doesn't look like pheasant to me either. But those're *huge* crows."

"What's the biggest crow?" Marty asked. "What's the record for the biggest crow? Maybe *I* should be in one of those books." He slammed his fist down on the toolbench. "Geez! I'll bet we should never have cut 'em up! Now nobody can tell how giant they were!"

Jut pulled out his book of records. "No crow records," he said after a search. "Bird records, but no crow."

"How's come? Crows're all over the place! What birds are more important than crows?"

"Chickens," Jut said, his head in the book. "And turkeys."

"Chickens?" Marty's voice was heavy with disgust.

"Don't make fun of chickens. This chicken named Weirdo weighed *twenty-two pounds.* Killed his own son, an eighteen-pounder."

Nick sucked in his breath. "Yow!"

"Yup," Jut continued. "Killed two cats, messed up a dog, and his owner had to have eight stitches." Grinning, Jut looked up from his reading. "That's some bird."

"Chickens," Marty said scornfully, "aren't wild game. There's a *difference.*"

"Yeah," chimed Nick, in surprise support of Marty.

"Let's go cook them," Jut said, shoving his book back into its pocket. "I told the guys on Holly Tree Court we'd have a ballgame later when Gus takes his nap."

Jut was washing pieces of crow in the sink when he heard his mother come up beside him. "Uh, hi," Jut said. He casually draped a paper towel over the bird pieces on the counter. His hands rested on those still in the sink.

Mrs. Howard lifted the paper towel. For a

minute she looked at the bird parts. She picked up a breast, turned it over to examine it, and laid it back down. "Pigeon?" she asked. "That's no pheasant. Anyway, I heard there wasn't going to be a season on pheasant. They've gotten too scarce."

"Crow," Nick said.

"Pardon me?" Mrs. Howard looked from Jut to Marty, who was thumbing through a cookbook. Marty didn't look up.

"CROW!" Nick hollered.

"Ssh, son," Nick's mother said. She look
at Jut, but she didn't say anything. She didn
have to.

Slowly, Jut nodded. He looked straight
ahead out the kitchen window and nodded.

"You're not kidding me?"

"We're not kidding you. Marty's a very good
shot. Dad'd be proud of him."

Mrs. Howard closed her eyes and sagged
slightly against the edge of the counter. "And
. . . uh . . . you are going to *cook* it, right?"
She turned to look at Marty and the open
cookbook.

"Right," Marty answered. He began to hum.
"Four and twenty blackbirds baked in a pie
. . . remember? A crow is a very black bird.
Should be delicious."

Nick sang, "When the pie was *ooooopened*,
the birds began to siiiiiinnnnnng! Wasn't that
a lovely dish to set before a kiiinnnnng!"

Mrs. Howard stood erect. "I, however, am
not a king. I am not even a queen or a prin-
cess. I am an average, humble, *insane* mother
of four!" She took a breath and rushed on.
"And I am not eating one bite of crow. I don't

even care if your feelings are hurt. I refuse to eat crow pie. Now, *good night.*" She turned and walked rapidly out of the kitchen.

Gus came into the kitchen soon after his mother's departure. Jut heard his mother's door shut and knew they had Gus for the afternoon. "Well," he told Marty, "she didn't slam the door."

"There isn't enough for five anyway," Marty said. "You brown the pieces in butter while I make this sauce. We can't put this crust on until they're almost done cooking. Slop 'em around in flour first, before you brown 'em, okay?"

"Crust?" Nick was a fan of pies and piecrust.

"Crust," Marty repeated. "It's a crow pie. Just like in the song, except ours aren't going to sing."

Jut floured the bird parts like Marty showed him and fried them for a while in butter. Beside him at the stove, Marty hummed and stirred things into a sauce.

"You *like* cooking, don't you?" Jut asked.

"Sure. Like you like basketball. Because it's fun." Marty put a pinch of dried parsley into his sauce.

"Sure it's fun," Jut said heavily. He had tried hard not to think about how much he wanted to make the basketball team. Most of the other boys in eighth grade wanted to be on the team, too. Tryouts were the end of the week. Jut was afraid he wasn't ready—would never be ready—no matter how much he and Amazon Brown worked.

When the various parts of browned crow were put into the casserole dish, Marty added his sauce. The smell was wonderful. Jut decided that Marty knew what he was doing, and slid the covered dish into the oven to bake.

"Little over an hour," Marty read in the cookbook. "That's for pigeon. Don't see why crow'd be any different. Then we put on the crust. Let's put Gus to bed and go play ball till the pie's ready."

"Will it be like cherry pie?" Nick asked.

"Will *what* be like cherry pie?" The cheerful, brisk voice filled the front hall and then the kitchen.

"Miss Brown?" Jut said in disbelief.

"That's me!" She set two large grocery sacks on the kitchen counter. "I finally thought of what I could do to make up to you guys for my rotten advice about the bees. You know," she said, looking at Marty, "that has really bothered me. You guys could have been hurt. Or your mom. Some nurse, huh?"

"It's all right. The bees were dopey, like you said. They wouldn't have hurt anybody. And you took us to a World Series game. That's plenty!" Marty gave the nurse a friendly smile. "What's in those sacks?"

"Dinner is in those sacks," she announced. *"Home-grown dinner."* Proudly she set her gifts on the counter: acorn squash, tomatoes, a huge pile of potatoes. The counter overflowed.

"Yeccchh!" Nick glowered at the squash.

"Marty, put Gus to bed now, okay?" Jut gave Marty a special look.

"But we have *already*—" Marty began, his hands gesturing toward the oven.

"Yeah, Marty, I know," Jut interrupted. "I'll fix it. Just take Gus up to bed, huh?"

Marty got the message. He picked Gus up off the floor. He had been playing in the pans and was still holding a lid as he was carried up to bed.

Amazon Brown sniffed the air in the kitchen. "I smell something good." Her face drooped. "Have you already fixed your Sunday dinner?"

"Yeah! And we *hate squash!*" Nick's voice was anything but grateful.

"Shut up, Nick!" Jut wished again that Nick would drop dead. He was always embarrassing people. "We only fixed the meat. Marty and I went hunting yesterday, that's why. So we made, ah, uh—a bird pie."

Miss Brown was cheered. "And we still need all the trimmings! Baked squash, stewed tomatoes, mashed potatoes. . . . Doesn't that sound delicious?"

"Stewed tomatoes?" Jut asked weakly. He *loathed* stewed tomatoes. They weren't fit for a dog. *Nobody* he knew ate stewed tomatoes.

"Just let me make the whole thing as a surprise. Take Nick and go play ball or something. Or ride your bikes. Get out of the house and leave the whole thing to me." She beamed at Jut.

Marty spoke from the doorway. "Okay, but I have to come back to finish my pie. We're gonna eat at four."

"Great! I'll be ready. And don't worry about a thing. This is *my present.*"

"Some present," Marty said gloomily on their way to Holly Tree Court. He beat the ground with his bat on every other step. "Some present."

"I don't even want to think about food," Jut said. "Yesterday we had that hunting lunch, and now this. I never knew food was such a problem."

"I HATE SQUASH!" Nick yelled, unable to stand it another minute.

"Me, too," Jut and Marty said together.

"Mom loves it," Jut remembered.

"*I* love baseball," Marty said. "Look, everybody's there already."

By four, everyone was back inside the house and ready for dinner. Gus was up from his nap and seated at the table in his highchair. Marty had set his bird pie in the center of the table. Steam rose from its pricked, browned crust. The smell was still wonderful.

Miss Brown was busily covering all the bare spots on the table with her vegetables. Sliced tomatoes sat next to baked squash, which was beside stewed tomatoes, which was next to mashed potatoes. "Should we get your mother up for dinner?" she asked.

"No!" chorused Jut and Marty. Jut added, "We never wake her up, not if we can help it."

"Can I put some pie on your plate, Miss Brown?" Marty had put a leg and sauce and crust on Nick's plate. He had given a thigh to Gus, who was already gnawing on the small piece of meat.

"Of course. I wouldn't miss it. The smell is heavenly." She sat down between Gus and Nick.

"It's kinda chewy," Nick said. His mouth was full of meat, and he was chewing steadily.

"Don't take such big bites," Marty told him. "That's being a pig."

"I *didn't*! And I ain't a pig!"

"Well now, it *is* a little firm," Miss Brown agreed. She chewed in a determined, regular motion and smiled at Nick. "But modern people are probably spoiled by tenderer meats than the pioneers. *They* were *used* to eating wild game. And it's very good for us. Nothing artificial, you see." She began chewing on another bite.

"This breast's pretty good," Jut told Marty. "Tastes a little like pheasant, doesn't it?"

"A little. But the pieces are pretty small. Crust is good, though, and easy. I used Bisquick."

"Num, num," Gus said.

Miss Brown heaped squash on her plate. She slid two slices of tomato onto Nick's plate. "You don't have to eat the squash, Nick, but please have tomato." She passed the serving plate of tomatoes to Marty. "What kind of fowl is this?" she asked him. "All this time I thought it was pheasant. What else is in season?"

"Crow," Nick said quickly.

Amazon Brown looked around the table, from Jut to Marty to Nick and last to Gus. Gus was eating mashed potatoes with his fingers.

"I beg your pardon," she said in even, precise syllables.

"CROW!" Nick repeated. "And it's not near as good as squirrel."

Marty nodded agreement. "You're right, Nick. Squirrel's a lot better and not as much work."

Miss Brown swallowed a noisy swallow. Her face was pained. "Crow?" she asked in a small voice.

"I'm afraid so," Jut began. He wasn't sure how he could ever explain why they were eating crow. How you had to eat what you killed. How he might never go hunting again.

"It's very hard to shoot a crow," Marty announced. "Farmers hate them, but crows're smart so you almost never get to shoot one. Unless you're quick and have a *lot* of patience."

The nurse nodded. She was leaning back against her chair and not eating. Not even the stewed tomatoes.

"Here," Marty said. "Have one of these big pieces of white meat. That's breast, and it's the best."

"Oh, my," she said quickly, one hand over her plate, "I don't want to take the best piece. That wouldn't be fair!" Her voice squeaked slightly.

"Sure it would. You brought us all your vegetables, so we'll share our pie with you." Marty smiled innocently.

Jut realized how terribly fair it was. She'd brought them stewed tomatoes and squash. They'd fed her crow. He wondered if he could keep a straight face.

"More shicken," Gus said, holding out his cleaned thigh bone. Gus called all meat "shicken."

Miss Brown cut a very, *very* tiny piece of meat off the breast and put it into her mouth. She added a large forkful of mashed potatoes and chewed.

Later, Miss Brown made them practice passing on the driveway court. "Low, and take careful aim," she warned. "You don't want the other guys getting *your* ball." Jut paid close attention. Tryouts were so close he could almost feel the weight of them.

A little later the nurse asked, "You guys don't really eat squirrels, do you?"

"Sure. Dad grew up on a farm in Iowa, and everybody that hunts there knows how good squirrels are." Marty passed a fast ball to Jut. "This was our first time for crow, though."

"I grew up in Detroit," Miss Brown said. "Nobody there eats squirrels. They try to tame them, feed them crackers and cashews, give them names. But *nobody eats them.*"

"That's weird," Nick said.

Jut decided he could laugh now. Now he could laugh all he wanted.

13

The Awful Smell

Jut pushed another thumbtack into the blanket and on down into the wood frame around the door. He and Marty were putting blankets across the two doorways of the living room. That would keep the smell *in* the living room. Or so Marty said. It was Marty's idea, and Marty said it just showed how helpful he was.

But when it came to the smell, nothing was helpful as far as Jut could tell. And, somehow, the smell was his fault. It hadn't ever happened before, had it? Only when *he* was in charge.

Nothing his mother said made him feel any better about the odor. She told him how impressive it was that everyone always had clean clothes, that the dishes were clean and in their cupboard, the pets watered and fed, the lawn neatly mowed. Everything important was being done and done right, she said. It was awful that they had fed crow pie to Miss Brown, but otherwise the food had been wonderful. Jut was to concentrate on basketball tryouts, his mother said, and forget about the smell.

But, of course, he couldn't forget. "Marty," Jut said a couple days before tryouts, "what're we going to *do* about the living room?"

Marty was quiet awhile before he answered. When he spoke he sounded very determined. "We'll just plain *sit* in there until we find the smell. We'll *brainstorm* it, that's what."

Jut nodded and felt a tiny bit better. He didn't know what he'd do without Marty.

After dinner that night, the family pushed aside the blankets and went into the living room. The blankets flopped back into place and there they were, sealed in with the smell.

"What did the library book say about this house? You did get it, didn't you?" Jut was ready to consider anything.

"Yes. Mrs. Petersen dropped it by on her way home yesterday afternoon." Jut's mother picked Gus up off the floor and held him on her lap. "The book said that our house is pretty much the same as when it was built, back in the 1840s. And they *think* it was part of the underground railway for escaping slaves. But they're not sure.

"There's a hidden wine cellar in the basement that they know about. We'll have to find that when your dad gets home." She looked at the oak panel. "But whether there's a room back there or not, nobody knows. This house sat vacant for a long time in the early 1900s, and information seems to have been lost then. But *we* know there's some kind of space behind there. We can *hear* it."

"Maybe like the wood cupboard," Jut suggested. He went over to the oak panel that stretched its length beside the fireplace. "Listen." He pounded at regular intervals across the panel. Just above the mantel was the dull, solid sound. Below, it was different.

Nick came close to listen. He pounded some himself. "Very suspicious," he said importantly. He sat down and leaned up against the panel as if it would help him to think. "Stinks worse here," he said.

"We know that, stupey," growled Marty. "Why do you think we want to know what's in there?"

"Martin," Mrs. Howard scolded, shaking her head.

Marty scowled at Nick. Nick put his hands in position and began to play his nose. Nick twanged his nose with a finger of one hand, while the other hand held one nostril shut. All the while he hummed a tune. The result was nasal, faintly musical, and very noticeable. Jut and Marty both hated it. Nick knew they hated it.

Jut looked at Nick and wished for the umpteenth time that his father were *home*. Not gone. Especially not in Europe, a place that had no reality. "Nick," he began, "do you *have* to—"

"Yep, I hafta," sassed Nick. He whirled around and laid down on his back on the floor. He put his feet up on the wood panel next to the fireplace and resumed playing his nose.

"Nicholas," Mrs. Howard said, "one more sassy remark out of you and you will march

upstairs to bed. Is that clear?"

"Yeah," Nick answered. His nose-playing volume decreased.

Jut sighed and rubbed a hand across his forehead. If this was Marty's idea of brainstorming, he wasn't sure he could take it for long. Only one hidden place, or so the book had said. A wine cellar. Did that mean there were *other* hidden rooms or cupboards in the house? Not for sure.

The nose-playing stopped abruptly and Jut raised his head. His breath caught while he watched the oak panel. *It moved.* Nick and Marty saw it moving. Mrs. Howard saw it.

And no one could say anything. As they watched, the panel creaked and protested, but it *moved.*

Jut looked at Nick's feet. Both of them were about twelve inches off the ground. One foot was pressed against the wood molding that ran between the fireplace and the tall oak panel.

It's his foot, Jut said to himself. There's some kind of spring. A secret spring just like in books. And it's been there all along, for over a hundred years.

Jut watched, rigid with excitement, as the panel slowly opened sideways. As the dark space on the left of the fireplace grew, so did the terrible smell.

"Looka that! Looka that!" Nick's voice broke the silence.

"Pew!" Gus said. "Big pew!"

"Right," breathed Jut, wanting to laugh like a crazy man. "It's a room, Marty! A secret room! Like the wood cupboard!"

"Two of everything," Marty said. "Just like we thought."

"And it isn't my fault," Jut said, almost to himself.

"What's that, Justin?" Mrs. Howard's eyes were glued to the panel.

"Miaow?" said the dark space.

"Did you hear something funny?" Marty pushed his glasses into place.

"Yeah. The secret room said *meyow*. I bet I know where Eleanore goes." Jut's smile was broad.

Then the panel stopped moving. Nick pressed his foot against the wood molding next to where the panel had been, but nothing happened. The panel stood almost at a right angle to the living room wall. Half of it was back in dark space, the other half projecting out into the living room.

"Miaooow," the space said again.

Instantly, Jut and Marty and Nick were on hands and knees peering into the space. "PEW!" Nick said. "What's *in* here?"

"I can't see," Jut said. "Marty, get the flashlight." He sat back on his haunches and tried not to breathe.

Nick still gazed into the cupboard while his eyes gradually adjusted to the darkness. He drew a quick breath. "Oh! You guys, *look!* It's *babies*. Eleanore had *babies* in here. Lots of 'em!" Nick crawled all the way to the back of the space.

"Ssss," Eleanore warned. She hunkered low over the newborn kittens.

"Ick! Yuck! You guys!" wailed Nick. "Somethin's yucky on my hands!" Loudly, Nick backed out of the cupboard. In the living room, where they could see, he held up his hands.

"Yecch!" Jut leaned forward to look at Nick's hands. "You found the stink, all right.

130

It's something dead in there."

Marty dashed in through the blanket doorway with the flashlight. He shone it into the depths of the secret room.

Nick, forgetting his hands, looked into the space with Jut and Marty. "It's dead mouses," he said mournfully. "See?" He pointed to a pile not far from Eleanore.

"Mice, Nicholas," corrected Mrs. Howard in a mechanical voice. "Eleanore cannot have babies. She's been spayed and she's sterile. She can't get pregnant."

Jut withdrew his head from the cupboard. "Want to bet on that?" He crooked a finger, urging her to come and have a look.

"No, thanks. Just get her out of there. Poor thing. Delivering all those babies all alone. How do you suppose she got *in* there?"

Jut shrugged and stood up. "I'll get a shovel and paper bag so we can clean up the mess. Eleanore must have put her food in there for when she had her babies. Only the food went bad."

"That woman lied to us," Mrs. Howard said. "She told us that Eleanore had been spayed.

She *lied* to get rid of her last kitten."

"Adults tell lies too?" Nick sounded relieved.

"Oh, yeah," Marty replied. "Great big ones." He grinned at his mother.

"And they're *supposed* to know better." Mrs. Howard was not smiling. "Go wash your hands, Nicholas. Martin, get Eleanore and those kittens out of there. Put her in the laundry basket with some old rags for padding. Put the basket up in my room, please."

Jut got busy with the shovel and cleaned all of Eleanore's rotten food out of the new room beside the fireplace. Then he took a can of disinfectant spray and sprayed the place where the dead mice had been.

Mrs. Howard sat on the sofa holding Gus while she watched everyone work. When the kittens went by, she petted each one of them. "They *are* cute," she said, softening. "But I am furious with that woman for lying to us."

After the kittens were settled upstairs, Nick showed how to press on the wood molding. He put his foot in place. Several squeaky protests later, the panel was back in its original position. Like it had always been. A flat oak panel next to the fireplace.

"Wait till I tell Mrs. Petersen at the library," Mrs. Howard said, still amazed. "She'll insist that we be part of the historic house tour from now on. This house *has* to have been part of the Underground during the Civil War."

"The smell is *gone*," Jut said. "And did you see how clean it is in here? Marty and I kept cleaning because we hoped we could find the smell." He thought he had never been so happy to be rid of anything. He drew a deep breath and couldn't even *imagine* a bad odor anymore. Hallelujah!

Just then the phone rang. Mrs. Howard looked at her watch and stood up abruptly, setting Gus on the sofa. "That should be your father. I'll do the talking this time, you guys. I'm going to keep the secret room a secret. Won't that be fun?" She hurried off toward the kitchen phone. "Jut? Put Gus to bed, please. All of you get in bed now. It's after nine."

"She's really ticked off, isn't she?" Marty said to Jut. With Gus, they were all going upstairs. Everyone had made the panel move open and shut, so now they were ready to go upstairs.

"I see what she means," Jut answered. "That lady didn't need to lie. We'd have taken Eleanore anyway and had her spayed ourselves. I think Mom's just grumpy because she's sick of being sick."

"How'd Eleanore get in there?" Nick asked.

"From the outside somehow, I think—probably an old, mostly closed entrance in the woods next to our yard." Jut's eyes lit up. "But I'll bet she kept *trying* to get in there from the living room. She smelled her old food and kept thinking she ought to be able to get in there somehow. But we ought to look in the woods. I'll bet there's a place to crawl down under the ground. And an old tunnel leading into the secret room."

"I oughta bring my class here for 'Show and Tell,' " Nick said. "How about tomorrow?"

"Wait till Mom gets better, dummy!" Marty hopped up the last two steps. "And we have to spray those hinges with silicone to make the panel open smooth and silent. Like in a good murder mystery." Whistling the death march, Marty went into his bedroom.

"Yeah! Jut, you know what you could do?" Nick dropped his sweatshirt on the bedroom floor.

"What?" Jut said as he stuffed Gus into his sleepers.

"You could hide all the good guys in our secret room till after tryouts. Then you'd make the team for sure, huh?"

"Is that all the better you think I am?"

Later, when they were in their bunks for the night, Jut told Marty what Nick had said. "It was pretty funny, Marty. He was serious." Jut sobered. "I wish *I* thought basketball tryouts were funny."

"It's this Thursday and Friday, isn't it?"

"Yeah." Jut looked at the moon's patterns on his ceiling and tried to tell himself not to worry. Everything was going great, when you thought about it, so why wouldn't tryouts go well, too? And in a couple weeks his dad would be home. Then he could relax forever. Especially if he made the team.

14

Jut Tries Out

"No, Jut. Hands like this," Amazon Brown moved Jut's hands so that he held the ball exactly as she showed him. "Remember, when you're ready to shoot, get your hands in position. *Think*. It's in the head, Jut. All of it's in the head." She stepped back to watch him practice.

It was late when they had dinner. The nurse had come for practice and insisted on staying to fix them another vegetable dinner. "It's terrible to live alone and love gardening," she had told them. "Wait till you taste my new squash casserole."

"I'll fix a few hot dogs," Marty had whispered to Jut, "while you guys practice. That way we'll have something decent to eat."

"I can't understand it," Miss Brown said later when they were cleaning up dinner. "You guys are all good-sized, and healthy. But you're eating like *birds.*" She made a face. "Forget I said that."

Jut laughed. Then he decided to tell her the truth. "We eat like birds only when we have squash and stewed tomatoes. Remember how we ate at the ballpark? You were just unlucky."

"Well, this is my farewell dinner. Your mom's doctor said I didn't need to come anymore because she'll be up about eight hours a day now. Her headaches are gone and her appetite's good. *She* likes my vegetables."

"We don't exactly *hate* 'em," Marty said politely.

"Yes we do," Nick said. But he didn't sound sassy and he was smiling. Since he had discovered the moving panel, Nick had behaved himself.

"Our dad's coming home next week," Nick told the nurse. "I'm gonna show him how I can make lay-ups and how I found the secret room."

Jut thought of how good Nurse Brown was, and how thoughtful. How they had counted on her for a lot of things. Before she left, he made her promise to come back and meet their dad.

And then it was night and Jut couldn't sleep because tryouts were the next day. No more waiting. No more chance to practice.

In the school gym, Jut and all of the other hopefuls for the junior high team met with Coach Williams. Jut wore his oldest pair of gym trunks and his lucky shirt. He lined up with the rest of the eighth-graders and looked around the gym. Only a few seventh-graders. They knew their chances were slim. But the gym was full of enormous eighth- and ninth-graders. Jut couldn't get over how tall some of them were.

Next to Jut in line was another eighth-grader, named Rob Teasson. Jut thought he'd make the team for sure. Rob was tall and he looked professional. He had on a matched set of shorts and T-shirt. Even his socks were coor-

dinated. And he had brand-new shoes.

"Okay, fellas. This afternoon is just to loosen you up, give you the feel of the gym. Tomorrow's tryouts will begin right here, same time. Today, we'll do drills at the basket, shoot some free throws, and get to know one another." Coach Williams threw basketballs out of a large, wheeled cart.

"Line up in groups of five. Come on, *move it*! You guys at the head of the lines, get a ball."

Jut got in a line with four other eighth-graders. Rob Teasson was at the head of the line, as though he thought he belonged there. Jut waited nervously, wishing he were home in his woods—looking for the secret tunnel into his house. His throat was dry and his eyeballs hurt. Tryouts were awful.

"How'd it go?" Marty asked him that night in bed.

"Not too bad. The coach said he needed only six or seven players this year, though. Some of those ninth-graders looked pretty good to me. And there's Rob Teasson. Except," Jut's voice grew more optimistic, "Teasson's not as good as I thought."

Morning came and brought Friday, the final day of basketball tryouts. Jut was glad it was going to be over at last.

But not over quickly, he learned. Friday seemed to last forever. The hands of the school's clocks didn't move around normally. They crawled—one lousy hour after another.

Jut wasn't hungry at lunch. He just wanted lunch to be finished so that afternoon would come, and three-thirty, and then it would finally be over. He thought back to June when he had first told himself he was going to practice so he could try out for the team. Well, he got his wish. He was trying out . . . anytime now.

"Okay, guys, line up in your groups. Just like yesterday. Howard, you go to the head of that line over there."

Jut felt his stomach become rock hard. He nodded at the coach and went to the head of the line. Rob Teasson looked over from the head of his line and smiled a superior smile.

Today, Rob's outfit was red and white, the school colors. With matching socks. Jut still wore his old shorts and lucky shirt.

Jut reached down and picked up a basketball. He put his hands in place just like she'd showed him. Amazon Brown. A great coach. *It's in the head,* he said softly to himself. *It's all in the head.*

"Howard! Start your line through the drill and keep it moving! This man plans to be home for dinner at five-thirty!" Coach Williams blew his whistle, and Jut dribbled toward the basket.

15

Jut Retires

Jut's mother smiled over her cup of coffee at Jut. "And what wouldst thou wish, O Magnificent One, for thy retirement dinner?"

"We ought to have something Dad likes, too," Jut said, his heart filled with generosity. "It'll be his welcome-home dinner, right?"

"Yes, but he's been gorging himself all over Europe. It's *your* dinner. You pick what *you* want, but not too tricky. I still get pretty tired at the end of the day."

Jut piled school books on top of his notebook while he debated what to ask for.

"Bye, bye," Gus said, waving a fist full of toast.

"Bye, Gus. Isn't Mrs. Thomas going to keep him anymore?"

"In the afternoons, for another week or so, bless her soul. Your dad and I will have to think of a reward for her for all her help. Maybe a castle in Spain."

Jut waved good-bye to Gus, who kept saying bye, bye like a broken record. "How about roast beef?" he said on his way out. "All these weeks, we never had roast beef."

"That's fine. You'd better hurry up, Jut. You're going to be late for school. Marty and Nick left five minutes ago."

Jut balanced his books on the counter by the door. "All this time," he said, "*nobody's* been late for school." He smiled at his mother. "See you after basketball practice."

Jut walked quickly to school. Even the thought of Miss Twilley's English test didn't bother him. Because after school was basketball practice. And after that, his dad would be home.

Being part of the basketball team was even better than Jut had imagined. He'd been to only four days of practice, but still it was great.

Even if I never get off the bench—well, hardly ever—it'll be just super, he thought happily.

The coach was one reason Jut liked being on the team so far. Coach Williams wanted every player to be as good as he could possibly be. He really cared about every member of his team. He swore, he yelled, he turned red in the face—and he cared. Jut decided he would love being a basketball coach like Coach Williams.

I could coach during the week, he thought, *and on the weekends I could work at a wildlife refuge.* He had first had the idea of helping to save endangered animals on the long walk home from Plattners' farm the day he'd gone hunting with Marty. He had thought about it off and on since then. The more he thought about protecting animals, the better he liked the idea. *I can take Pierpont with me,* he decided, *as company.* The thought of Pierpont slogging along beside him through the tall grasses of a refuge made Jut laugh out loud. What with one thought and another, he nearly missed being in his seat when the bell rang.

Miss Twilley rapped her pencil sharply against the edge of her desk to get everyone's attention. Jut told himself that it looked like things were getting back to normal.

Mr. Howard's homecoming created a tremendous and wonderful commotion. Everybody talked and hugged all at once. Pierpont, who never bothered to bark, barked. Not once, but many times. During the homecoming-and-retirement dinner, he lay with his muzzle across Mr. Howard's feet.

Before the dinner, Nick dragged his dad into the living room to see the moving wood panel and the secret room. Marty shone the flashlight all over its walls. Mr. Howard was so dumbfounded he just shook his head over and over. "You guys," he kept saying, "you guys are really something."

"Of course," Nick agreed smugly. "There's a teeny little hole in the woods, too, Dad. That's where Eleanore got in to the secret room. We just found it yesterday, and Marty and Jut say it's really a big tunnel and we're gonna dig it open and you can help if you want."

"Big pew," Gus said, even though the smell had been gone for several days.

Eleanore, who had been keeping to her basket upstairs, entered the living room with one kitten in her jaws. It was a tiny calico girl kitten. She deposited it on Mr. Howard's left foot and stood back to watch his admiration.

"This, too?" Jut's father smiled. "Never a dull moment, right?"

"Right," Jut said in return. He hadn't said much yet. He especially hadn't said anything about his mother's sickness. He figured she'd tell him when she got ready. He thought his dad looked great, though. He could tell that the trip had been a success.

At the big dinner, most of the past few weeks came out. Marty told about the bees and Amazon Brown's bad advice that made all the bees come inside. Nick told his father that the grocery store was loaded with lots of things they never got to eat. Mr. Howard said, "Who's this Amazon Brown person I keep hearing about?"

Jut felt his turn had come. At least he figured that somebody ought to tell the good things.

"You should see her shoot free throws," Jut

told his father. "Always the same. Exactly. Just like a machine."

"And so she coached you guys after taking care of your mother?"

Jut noticed that he was holding Mrs. Howard's hand. And that the food on his plate was untouched.

"If I smile any more," Jut's mother said, "my face is going to crack." She continued to smile anyway, especially at Jut's father.

"Miss Brown took us to a World Series game against the Yankees, and she was always helping us with basketball. And she took us to two movies. Except for hunting day, she took us somewhere almost every Saturday," Jut said.

"Her squash stinks," added Nick.

"She's nice," Marty said loyally.

"And *you* made the team," Mr. Howard said to Jut.

"Sure did." Jut grinned. He thought how good it was not to be the father anymore. To have his own father back home.

Mr. Howard kept shaking his head in disbelief. "You'd think I'd been gone *five years* from all that's happened here. Jut, I believe you've earned a new pair of basketball shoes. Any pair in the store." He stretched his hand across the table to shake hands with Jut.

"Super, Dad. I can use a new pair. But you stay *home* now, okay, and you play *father* and I'll play *son*. I'm good at that."

"Oh, I'd hate to promise that," his dad said, trying hard to sound serious. "Now that you all know how to run the place, it would be a shame not to use those talents." He couldn't cover his smile any longer.

Jut grinned weakly. "But we could give them a nice, long rest, those talents. Couldn't we?"